An Early Frost: A Collection of Contemporary Ozark Short Stories

With great care and gentle urging, Jory Sherman helps us enjoy todays Ozarks. He explores the long held traditions of independent life and romantic living while reminding us that events in. the Ozarks can be brutal and unforgiving. He forces us to confront the Ozarks--by allowing us to discover that, like few regions, the past, present, and future all simultaneously exist.

The author, Jory Sherman, has interspersed his very successful career as a western writer (125 novels) with writings about his home of the last ten years, the Ozarks. His writings about the Ozarks have appeared in numerous newspapers and magazines. He is a hunter with both bow and muzzleloader, and a fisherman. Sherman lives with his wife, Charlotte, also a writer, and their son, Marc, in Forsyth, MIssouri.

AN EARLY FROST

By

Jory Sherman

For Art Dewey —
Some memories of the
Ozarks — and Happy New
Year! Best,

Jory Sherman

White Oak Press
Reeds Spring, Mo.

5 Jan. 1990

Pale in her fading bowers the Summer stands,
Like a new Niobe with clasped hands,
Silent above the flowers, her children lost,
Slain by the arrows of the early Frost.

Richard Henry Stoddard
ODE

An Early Frost:
A Collection of Contemporary Ozark Short Stories

By

Jory Sherman

White Oak Press
P.O. Box 188
Reeds Spring, Mo. 65737

DEDICATION

this book is humbly dedicated to
the memory of the late Dan Saults:
conservationist, outdoorsman,
environmentalist and writer -
and to his widow, Helen Saults.

An Early Frost

Table of Contents

INTRODUCTION

This is a gentle land, full of gentle people. But the Ozarks region is also a place that knows violence. Its borderland has seen bloody deeds since it was first settled almost 150 years ago. Passions can boil over here, as they can in other places. But this is not a history, nor an indictment. Rather, these brief glimpses of people and places here in these green hills are merely one man's observations, filtered through his own senses.

These are sketches of some of the Ozarkers I've encountered in nine years of living here. There are places and people here that I encountered as I roamed these hills, fished the lakes and streams, hunted the woods. Some of the people I have met here have been fictionalized, their identities disguised, for obvious reasons. That is the artist's prerogative and I have chosen to present their stories in this way in order to capture the essence of the Ozarks hills and its people.

When we moved here from California, we did not know anything about the Ozarks. But, the first people we met made us feel welcome. That was the wonder. The people. People make things work. My interest is in what moves through people, however, and that is why I try to observe them closely, listen to them. The very few things I know, people taught me, showed me, and long ago it struck me that there was light in them and that it was the same light that came from the universe, from the mysteries we do not understand, the eternal drum of life in leaves and trees and rocks and rivers, things of the blood and heart that we cannot see, but are there.

I write for a living, but more than that, my writing affords me the chance to look into things and to see clearly. The Ozarks writings are done out of love, not for subsistence. They are a way of giving back invaluable, unmeasurable things that were given to me on special occasions: during a sunset of fire, a misty morning, in the woods, on the lake, or floating down a river. Special times when the mind is clear and this good earth opens up like a flower.

I write, too, in order to understand what it is that I see, and feel. And, if it's possible to convey a small particle of these things, the intuitions, the conclusions, the mysteries, then my purpose has been accomplished. Yet, the pieces in this book are merely fragments, attempts to paint some things I saw and felt and tried to capture in words.

These are sketches, not portraits.

They are, I hope, impressions that I tried to write down truly, using only the simple materials at hand: my eyes, my heart, my hands. There is death here, as there is death in a lot of other places. But each society handles this part of life somewhat differently. Death is a part of life, just as birth is. Each person, as each society, handles this aspect of living in different ways, at different times.

The scenes in this book are not photographs.

They are only blurred scrawls, notes made in passing, echoes of people I met and who told me some few fragments of their lives.

An Early Frost

They are not responsible for these words here, but they are the ones who made me search for the words to describe them with my limited ability.

Thank you, all of you, for letting me walk through your fields, fish your ponds, sit at your tables, listen to your talk, rock on your porches, take from your gardens.

There are seasons we must face, changes in the earth, ravages dealt by time and the weather, scars we must bear in our journey through life. The hills are not always verdant, the fields not always abundant with clover, but turn sere and lifeless under the beat of August's sun. The harvest sometimes falls victim to an early frost, the pumpkins shrivel up and die on the vines, the apples wrinkle and wither before they can be plucked. But still I walk the orchards and valleys, the hills and hollows, fish the streams and ponds and lakes of mighty country and feel full with it, happy to have seen what I have seen, what you have let me see. You have let me see into your hearts, as I roamed these green hills of your home and on into the autumn chill of your lives. What is written here is written for the sake of memory, that these lives that touched me will not be forgotten. The sketches that follow represent some of what I have seen of life and death in these Ozarks hills. They are, I hope, a celebration of life, even when dealing with physical death. For I believe in man's spirit. I believe that spirit lives forever.

Jory Sherman
Forsyth, Missouri

FOXFIRE MIST

Only the morning was alive.

The dawn boiled up in a swirl of light without sun or source, a turbulent alchemy of cool stream swallowing rocks and trees and earth as if King Arthur's mad Merlin himself had uttered a cloaking spell over the land.

I walk lorn along the Ozarks road next to the wounded woods.

The first snows of this winter have fallen, the previous day, cloaked the earth with a majestic ermine dust, thick as heapings of refined sugar. During the night, a faint thaw breathed away some of the snow, warmed rocks and tree trunks so that patches of bare earth blotch the albino landscape.

The temperature quivers below freezing, still, but it is oddly warm, as if that hot thaw southern breath is still puffing out of a gulf furnace, razing the crystalline banks of snows with invisible currents that knife the vagrant chill which prowls the winter morning.

The mist enfolds like a warming cloak and the brave cedars have deadened the wind with their evergreen gloves. The deer tracks have left wide cicles in the snow, muddy clefts that are frozen into cuneiform tablets a man might read and understand.

It is quiet and the earth itself seems empty at this vacuous hour. My heartbeat thrums as loud as fear itself. There is no one here. I am alone and the mist is suffocating.

The fine quality of the morning out here is its vacancy, its utter indiffrence. It does not matter if I am here or not. The trees don't care; the earth is like a mighty Sphynx underfoot, sleeping for eternities regardless of intrusions.

The light, though, begins to take a shape of its own. It assumes the motion of arabesquing mists, assimilates the forms of these earthclouds that smother the land with a kind of primordial reminder of the legendary Void.

The light--it takes my breath away, gives it back. Foxfire, they call it. A mystical radiance that slinks out of the lowlands and sniffs under bridges, hugs the mossy feet of trees and searches through empty fields at dusk and early of a morning. A faery light spoken of in whispers by oldtimers who recall the bogs and moors of the old country and see the mirrored reflections of those ancient anglican nations in these Ozark hills.

When I think about these things and realize that the earth, this mist, doesn't care, isn't malevolent or dangerous, I am no longer afraid. Rather, I feel as if I was back in San Francisco, under a streetlamp bathed in brume. It's like being up on Russian Hill or down along the Embarcadero, near the mindless sea, the Jack London-haunted bay.

This mist seems to come from such a sea. The comforting, ever-changing, restless sea. The time beach where we floated to shore so long ago when we could not see land or tree or rock. It's as if the good Gulf air had come to the

Ozarks for a brief visit, bringing us a reminder of eternity and infinity, of the Void that once was.

When I was a small boy, I used to think of that void, that awesome nothingness. I must have heard of it in Sunday school class or read about it in a book. Or dreamed it. I pictured it in my mind. The universe was an egg and the egg was empty. It was a very frightening image. It is frightening now, in a cosmic sense. To think of a place, a whole vast place, that was absolutely nothing at all, that was, according to Genisis, "without form, and void; and darkness was upon the face of the deep. And the Spirit of God moved upon the face of the waters."

I was awed then and I am still awed when I think about total nothingness, a noneness that is almost incomprehensible.

The mist hangs here, strays, lingers, hovers, drifts, for a long time. The light, the foxfire light, builds, explodes, permeates, invades the delicate showdowswirl of these steamclouds. It is like being alive at the dawn of creation. It is like being present during the time of the inexpresible Void and seeing nothings take shape. First, perhaps, a fine mist, and then a mass, pulsing with heat, with energy. Or maybe only a thick soup, sometime after the beginning of things, flooding through nothingness and breaking up into fiery chunks that gradually cooled as that mysterious force, gravity, held the newly created solids in perfect check and balance.

I know that none of this was simple. Yet, we have a clue or two to guide us in our search for how matter was created, is created. Not, specifically, as the King James translation of the Bible says, from the Word, but from the thought. The big thought. The beginning of everything is thought. A mind conceiving something from nothing. That is simple enough, but not accurate enough. The thought must have energy. That energy is belief. To believe a thing will occur, will be created, and to believe that such a thing is already created, is the secret to all creation. These stray thoughts of mine, as I stroll through a small world of mist and cloud, bring these points home to me.

Yet, complex as my world is, as simple as it appears, I realize that its existence is beyond my comprehension. But it was within

Someone's comprehension. Francis Crick, the Nobel Prize winner who wrote Life Itself, Its Origin and Nature, in trying to explain the barely fathomable world of DNA and RNA, wrote this: "An honest man, armed with all the knowledge available to us now, could only state that in some sense, the origin of life appears at the moment to be almost a miracle, so many are the conditions which would have had to have been satisfied to get it going."

What is life and why is life? These are questions that echo in my mind as I walk through the creation of morning. And I do not take this morning for granted. I am present at its creation after all, and there must be something to learn here. Yet, it is probably arrogant of me to assume so much from such scanty evidence as clouds, mist and a strange, seldom seen light.

I do not want to make too much out of these small moments. They are normal, I suppose, for this time of year and for this place. But, somewhere inside me is a child who remembers his first primitive thoughts, his first fears, his first inklings that once there was nothing and now there is everything. Will someone come along and take it all away? That was the childhood fear. If there was nothing once, there could be nothing again.

Someone has described me as an immigrant to the Ozarks. I suppose that is technically so. Yet I have never felt like an immigrant. Not that there is any adverse connotation to the term. It is true that I was not born to these parts and I am a relative stranger. But, when I came here, I did not feel that I was an intruder nor an outlander. Rather, I felt that I was coming back home.

This is a complex feeling, but I guess I mean that this was the place I had always wanted to be, without actually knowing where it was. I knew that such a place must exist, but I had never been there.

I am here now. I no longer feel like an outsider. Nor an immigrant. Yet, this morning, in foxfire mist, with the light swirling through gauzeclouds of an uncertain origin, I realize that I am still coming into the Ozarks, into this good earth, to find something that I dreamed of as a child. A place where I could see creation happen; where I could search through what memory I was given to look for my beginnings. To look for a Father. A Great Spirit.

There will be light today and the mists will drift away. At the end of the road, I turn back toward home. Certain trees I had not seen earlier will be visible now. Some will be gaunt and leafless. The cedars will give off their musty scents, their eerie green-black glow. I will look again at the wedges of deer tracks and remember a clay tablet in a museum that had an important message left behind for us to decipher.

As the mist rises, I will wonder where it is going, why it was here. And I will guess at where it came from. Don't talk to me about convection and air currents. Tell me about faeries and gossamer-winged creatures that seek out the eerie lights that surge through these hills on magical mornings and lurk in the shadows on certain dusks when the moon is hidden behind dark clouds and the woods turn invisible as if swallowing the earth, as if returning it to the void from whence it came.

Talk to me about things that make sense for a romantic who immigrated to these Ozark hills to find the answers to all those boyhood questions that seemed to have no earthly source.

Tell me what you see in these mists, if you dare, and tell me the true meaning of creation and the peculiar light that natives call "foxfire."

THE COMING OF SPRING

Some days here, you can sense the coming of spring to these Ozarks hills. There is the urgency of the morning tapping at your mind with the insistence of crickets. There is the dawn itself, with its ruddy cheeks, its promise of a long day's sun. This special dawn is more confident, healthier, stronger, livelier than it was during the long winter.

The morning, on these sweet Ozarks days, shrugs its shoulders like a young child. You can feel the warm smile of the day on your face when you open the door. April rushes up to you on a girl's silver skates and sprays you with a splash of icy breeze delicate as a silken shawl. A deep breath tastes of cedar and redbuds and dogwood blossoms. The lake breeze is fresh, bright as sleek trout moving in shallow creek waters.

A once-dry creek bed fills with snow melt, breaks through a deep hollow, wends its way along the thawed ground seeking life and the mingling with the big lake that was once a mighty river. The bluffs, still frigid with ice and secrets, catch the warming sun, reluctantly shed their long ermine beards, become shawls of dripping waterfalls. You can hear the water's ancient song long into the night.

Spring in the Ozarks is fickle, relentless, full of surprises. It brings out the raccoons, the opossums, the brown robber birds. Gray squirrels skitter down the oak trees with flaring paramesium tails and chittery voices. The air soars across the newborn land, full of promises and pleasant whispers.

This is the way Spring is for me here. This is the way it moves in and heads for summer. This is the way it sings its green songs, weaves its gold sun threads during its time of birthing. It is awesome in its quietness, splendid in its muscling youth. You can't help but feel the continuity of the universe, the perfect rhythms beneath the seeming chaos, the symmetry of life itself.

A man doesn't need much more than this.

THE BUTTERFLIES

One day I saw a butterfly float through the woods on golden wings. Free of the cocoon and winter, he fluttered across the land in a scurry, threading an invisible flight path in the warm spring sun, like a dancer having nothing to do, showing off his new wings. Two weeks before, I saw his brother, too early for spring, perched on a broken branch clustered with cedar sprigs that had fallen to the snow.

Thinking it alive and resting from its flight, I stooped down to look at the creature more closely. It didn't move. My hand reached out to touch its wing and I saw its feet were fastened to the branch. It had been frozen there, its wings spread wide. Perfectly preserved, it looked as though it had been waiting for the cold to pass.

I brought the butterfly home, still locked to its foothold on the browned cedar branch, and set it on one of the bookcases.

The quick and the dead, the one aflight, skimming on the warm zephyrs of Cedar Creek, the early butterfly caught in the chill, as though pinned to the earth midway in its course by a lepidopterist. I take no meaning from these things, but only marvel that some beings fly and some are stiffened by the late, hanging-on winter.

The butterflies must have a time clock inside them that tells them it is time to break free of the branches and head for open spaces. Nature sometimes plays the fickle lady and taunts her delicate charges with the whispering lips of death.

This is what happened with the frozen butterfly. He was no less the flying dancer, but he looked up at blue skies over the lake and felt the warmth of a cloudless day too soon. Eager fellow, anxious to strut and show off his bright yellow wings, he became that year's Icarus of the forest, a victim of unperfected cryogenics.

An Early Frost

The butterfly will never come alive again, never dance on the air, never fly above the gelid perch where he last drew breath.

The one who waited, the one I saw dazzle his way above the still snowy earth might make his way into summer. I hope he does. He has my heart in his wings. He flitted away like an old movie, into infinity, his body growing smaller and smaller until he finally winked out of sight.

There is really no vocabulary to explain such things. It's just that we all have a quirk about life and sometimes life has a quirk about us. The butterfly that flew away is just as gone as the one that I placed on my bookcase. I see them both equally in the tapestry of life. Both are vivid in my mind, both are real. Both are gone.

Butterflies now give me a very strange feeling. Life is so ephemeral, for them and for us.

I wish I could explain how I feel about them. I wish they could explain about me.

TWILIGHT

From this hill above the hollow we have a private view of a constantly changing painting. This painting is not a canvas, but is composed of a minuscule portion of the Ozarks. There are far bluffs standing majestic above the tamed river that is now Bull Shoals Lake. There are two ridges converging on the lake, and the lake curves into infinity. The lake, in its day-life, assumes many colors and builds the fog-clouds that hide its long-kept secrets.

There is a dusk here like no other.

The lake accepts it and reflects its strange light like a mirror of time, like the surface impression of eternity. Now that the boats and fishermen have gone, now that the wind is down, it seems to be fashioned of bright metal for a moment as the last glow of sun limns the high ridges.

An Early Frost

In a while, the lake will be hammered into dull pewter, the last image of this corner of earth to give up its light. Yet now, the lake is fair of face, tranquil in its many depths, calm and confident of its own existence, its special swirl of timeless electrons.

The dusk begins building its shapes, its shadows, even as the last light hangs on, as the sun glides to a point between two peaks where it will blaze brilliantly one last time this day.

The deer move from the bedding grounds, now, to the hardwoods. The crackle of snapped twigs reveals their movement above the hidden creek below our back porch. A whippoorwill tunes up, its fluting trills muffled by the leafed-out trees. A neighbor's rooster crows in the distance, its disembodied voice echoing along the hollow. A thousand frog voices punctuate the echoes with an amphibian suddenness, a startling sound that carries over miles and centuries of water and earth. In the deeps, the fish swim like metal beings, silent, invisible.

Over the hills, acres of trees bleed olive-drab shadows from one last shot of sun.

Twilight

The lake is now a shimmering swirl of colors. On the porch here, a final bounce of light before fingers of dark touch, take hold. In the brush, a squirrel scurries to the safety of an oak before the predators prowl and float. There is a quietness now, of life, of death.

Twilight comes on fast. The world seems to settle as for sleep. The contours of the land blur and gentle as though a hand has smoothed the earth. The lake takes on the shadows of the bluffs. The trees draw back from the retreating light, greying with sudden age. The woods are full of whispers.

Dimness and susurrous, the frogs suddenly still, the littoral life quiet for a moment as the sun falls away finally this day. You can hear your heart beat, your own breathing, feel your pulse swell with the tide of deeper things beyond this moment.

In the backwash of this silence, an emptiness and a fullness: vestigial memories like the pages of bibles, the incomprehensible markings on scrolls and clay tablets, the scent of earthen jars, glimpses of cave paintings, inklings of far space, and mysterious beginnings.

An Early Frost

Now that the twilight is here, I can understand some places I have been, some awesome sunsets I have lived through: west Texas jackrabbits romping through backlit evenings in dusty sage landscapes turning orange, catching fire, stripebreasted Chukars whirring over rugged desert hills, owls floating off the carrier-decks of trees, doves landing in a whistle of wings on trembling tree branches, ducks falling into a pond like autumn leaves.

This is a good time to be alive. This is a good place to see and feel the night coming on. You can walk here without fear. In the big cities where the false lights come on automatically, your throat tightens, your stomach knots up, and you pull the curtains to shut out the nameless dread that rises up from the concrete, crackles in neon tubes like the frail bodies of electrocuted insects.

For a long moment, just before this corner of the world is drenched in darkness, there is a timelessness about everything the senses can grasp. There are no people, no sounds. There is no sign of civilization. There is only a deep hush, the dust of day hanging in the pale afterglow sky.

The sky turns dark, a lone star winks on.
It is very quiet now, very beautiful.
The transition is complete. Perfect.
And, somehow, eternal.

TAKING A WALK

I have been down through the woods again on a rain-sodden day. There was a sound, through the trees, like a mighty river roaring. The wind was up, booming this illusion through the hollow, as if the earth here was shaped like a huge sea shell that magnified certain vibrations in the ear; the blood coursing through veins, the throb of the heart muscle, the silence itself.

What is here for me among these newly leafed-out May trees? My boots sink into the mud-sog, touch hard stone. It seems so desolate here, so bereft of life. As if the hanging-on winter had stopped the breathing of creatures, imprisoned them in some kind of hibernative somnolence long after the sun finally found its way through the clouds.

Walk

There is something here. There is life. Some of it invisible. In the wind, a pulse, a scent, a hint of deer bedded down, squirrels in their dens, quail under brush, in soft wallows. Rabbits hiding in stony crevices, noses twitching, whiskers quivering.

How do we find such places as these? Why do we come here, stay? There are other places; maybe places just as good.

Somewhere, here in these thickening woods, there are answers. It is enough now to stop and touch a tree. There is energy in its trunk, in the tactile sensation of its rough bark. There is a message in the pattern its limbs form against the sky. Shapes, outlines, patterns, frames. Something to sketch in thoughts that crowd the mind, some good empty spaces to search through for whatever may be found: answers, perhaps; meaning.

Stopping here, I am conscious that something is breathing in these woods besides myself. The trees breathe, of course. Oxygen is poison to them, so they expel it, as I expel carbon dioxide. One's waste is another's need. The rocks are alive, too, formed of the same star-dust as everything else on this planet, the fine silt of long-ago explosions when there was only Void. And, now, I sense the rocks and trees, myself, pulsing with the same vital rhythm that courses through the entire universe.

I think Gustav Mahler, and the sobbing plod of percussive patterns forming a backdrop to the brassy, soaring horns, the strings all fighting for a foothold in the Fifth Symphony. Here, in the apparent silence, I hear the bugling of ancient hunting horns in a sylvan glen; the distant baying of hounds on an English moor.

It is so solemn here, that music rises up out of the morning dankness, some of it soft and slow, some bright allegro.

Back up the hill, at the house, I can hear the wind chimes on the front porch, delicately melodic. Man-made, these pipe-bells seem oddly apropos here, faintly Oriental. They make clear pure sounds like fine crystal struck with a silversmith's hammer.

I walk on, out of earshot, beyond the reach of the wind chimes, deeper into the woods, beyond the gurgling, rainy weather creek. A friend tells me there ought to be morels up in the hardwoods, or in the cedar stands where the grass grows a thin carpet in cool shadows. But, I have been to these places and the wild mushrooms still elude me. There is something mystical about these little fungus creatures. Someday, maybe my timing will be right. Maybe I'll find a sackful. I looked early this year, and late, and while I saw a few edible varieties, they either grew too high, on trees, or were too few to bother with, singles, no bigger than marbles.

The walk is rugged, takes me in no particular direction. I get my second wind and there is Bull Shoals beyond this meager creek that flows so seldom. I cross over, again, climb the steep slope to a grove that has been partially cleared by woodcutters. There is a seeping spring here, and more grass growing under cedars. Not a morel to be seen. But, I can hear the squirrels now, and a bob white quail piping in a neighbor's meadow. There are deer rubs on a sapling or two. There is life all around me, in me.

Ralph Waldo Emerson, who saw very deeply into things, once wrote that "the first care of a man settling in the country should be to open the face of the earth to himself by a little knowledge of Nature, or a great deal, if he can; of birds, plants, rocks, astronomy; in short, the art of taking a walk."

Well, I have taken a walk, and I have opened up the face of the earth. Some of it, anyway. There was a moment or two back there, when I felt I could have stayed forever in the woods. Now, breathless, back at the house, I look at the front porch, see the wind chimes tink, hear again the faint music. I am glad the house is here, in this good place.

I am glad the woods are out there and that I can walk them in my search for a little knowledge of Nature.

THE SUMMER PEOPLE

June gentles the land with sun. The ridge between the old Forsyth ferry and Kirbyville greens itself like some farmer's field, the oaks and cedars blazing emerald from dawn to dusk. The valleys beyond the old freight road seem like a fairyland in morning, the hills rising like islands, the far ones bathed in a gossamer mist like the smudged underpainting of an artist's canvas.

The morning lake is still, a sheet of polished steel snaking to a point miles away, where it disappears like the ghost of the river it once was. A few moments ago, my dawn whippoorwill moved close to the open bedroom window, filling my room with his piercing, high-pitched cries. He sounds like a maddened flutist stuck on the same notes, and he sounds, too, like a friend who just happens to sing in a foreign language. At my neighbor's, across the hollow, a rooster crows.

The whippoorwill goes silent suddenly, as if the cock's crow signalled a fatal sunrise. I have never seen this bird whose cry is so loud for a few brief moments, but only his shape, silhouetted among the leaves of an oak tree. He is only a shadow to me, without form, isolated, the source mysteriously hidden somehow. He comes when the world goes to sleep, and he does not leave until the woods awaken.

A grey squirrel chitters at my shape in the window, furling and unfurling his tail like a quilled flag. He is young, bold, and I wonder if he has seen the whippoorwill or only a shadow streaming across his tree branch before it disappears in the silence of the deep woods. I wonder where the whippoorwill goes.

On Lake Taneycomo, as the sun rises, the first boats pull away from the shore, chug up toward Table Rock Dam through low fog. The men who work the docks on Bull Shoals are busy, the fishermen still sleepy-eyed, impatient to head for the sunken trees where the crappie lurk, or the sandstone banks where the bass hide. Table Rock Lake, too, is teeming with fisherfolk who want to beat the sun to their favorite spots. A pair of farmboys, barefooted and cutoffed, trip to the pond after catfish, lugging a can of squirming nightcrawlers, carrying poles with hook and line, clutching stringers and cans of pop.

Branson, Hollister, Forsyth, the villages near where we live, and all those along the tourist roads, from Kimberling City to Eureka Springs, like movie sets being prepared for a day's shooting, open up, as if someone was pulling open the giant doors of a sound stage. The whisper of brooms and the rattle of door locks crackle down the streets; the dusters and sweepers and Windexers urgently spiffing up their shops for the summer people of Ozarks Mountain Country.

The family driving up the last steep hill in their station wagon can feel the magic coming on as they look up at the bluffs. With their windows open, they can smell the fragrance of the countryside, see the acres of trees across endless hills. You can almost hear what they are saying. "Will one week be long enough to

see everything?" "What shall we do first?"
"Why didn't we come here before?" "Why
didn't we leave earlier?"

In the back seat, the children make their
wishes known. "I want to go horseback riding."
"Can we go to White Water first, Daddy?" "I
want to stay a whole day in Silver Dollar City."
These are just some of the conversations in all
those out-of-state cars streaming down from
Springfield, or up from Harrison, Arkansas on
Highway 65, or along the cross- threading 86
and 13 and 248 and 76 roadways (there are
more, of course!). These are just snatches of
private communiques floating on the heady June
air.

So, for some of us it is truly summer. The
sleds are stacked darkly silent under the back
porch, the hunting rifles oiled and put away for
the season, tents and camping gear dragged out
of the loft or the storage closet, airing out for
a trip to one of the campgrounds that border
the string of impoundments that form the lakes:
Beaver, Table Rock, Taneycomo, Bull Shoals,
Norfolk and so on down the line deep into
Arkansas.

Summer People

The summer people flow here, towing their boats, little toy cars behind monster motorhomes, swaying in their pickup campers, driving mere cars, with luggage racks loaded with canvas and Coleman stoves. They become part of the permanent Tri-Lakes community for a brief time that sometimes seems endless. They come on weekends and stay over extra days. They take their two weeks with pay and come to a place where time doesn't matter, a place with the oldest hills in America, the richest earth, the sweetest air. They take off their ties and their tailored suits, their chic city dresses and nylons and high-heeled shoes, trading them in for shorts and T-shirts and sandals.

It's Mauna Loa time and Acapulco afternoons, Rive Gauche strolls with blossoms scenting the air. It's spectacle, the changing of the guard at Buckingham Palace, Fiating over the Pyranees and through vinyard-laced Italy, catching the bullfights at Pamplona on Sunday at four o'clock in the afternoon, bumping elbows with brownskinned Filipinos along the Escolta in Manila, sipping a Daiquiri in San Juan.

An Early Frost

This Ozarks country is a place for summer people. It always was, even for the Indian tribes who swam the creeks and fished the mighty river that once coursed through this vast green valley.

I was one of the summer people once.

I came here, like you, and heard the whisper of older times, heard the faint talk of pioneers settling in places where the Osage Indians camped in summer over a hundred years ago. I heard the clang of axes ringing through the hardwoods, saw images of the roughhewn cabins going up, glimpsed the cooking fires searing fresh-killed meat, listened to the guitars playing plaintive on clear summer nights, discovered my own heart beating in time to this ancient tugging rhythm.

We stayed here, after being drawn back time after time, for no explainable reason, knowing this was where we wanted to be.

This is a place to stay, all right.

And, if you go away, some of this summer will linger with you all your days. You may find yourself returning again and again, as a visitor or in your thoughts. You may even find yourself trying to explain, as I am, why the summer seems so much richer here in the Ozarks.

You might even become, as we, one of the summer people who stayed on, perhaps destined to spend all the rest of life's seasons here, among these gentle hills.

THINGS OF BEAUTY

Memory.

As long as memory lasts, there is no aging, no death.

There may even be something to pass on to those who come after, to our children, our grandchildren, to people who will be born when our generations have been forgotten. If we put down the things we remember, we may even leave something of ourselves to other minds, other generations.

We may leave a collection of ideas and ideals, distinctions of character, morals. Or heritage.

We may just leave scraps of memory.

Memories of beautiful things we saw in passing.

The Ozarks have given much to me, to my family. I cannot speak for them, except that my wife, my sons and daughters, as well as those I've met here, are part of those memories. My memories.

Memories of beautiful things that are so fleeting, so ephemeral, they almost didn't stick in my mind. Almost.

Sometimes, those brief glimpses into a peoples' character, scenes of incredible beauty, leave a more lasting impression on the mind's memory than those things we see so often they dull our senses.

But, we must remember these things, and perhaps, we must record them lest they fade from what someone will someday call our heritage as a people, as humans who lived here for a brief time in these gentle hills.

Here are some of the impressions I've had that made no sense at the time, but only left me dumbstruck, somewhat awed. They are all simple things, everyday things, but they must mean something, because they move out of my mind now and onto paper with an urgency, a compelling urgency, to record them for now and whatever future is left to us.

An Early Frost

I don't know what they mean. Perhaps nothing. But, they may mean something to someone, or they may trigger the memories of others who will add to them, realize their place in time, in history.

They mean something to me, only because I feel fortunate to have glimpsed them, to have seen beyond myself, into lives not my own.

Beautiful things.

Things that float on the memory like ghost images, blurred and wavery photographs in an album.

Things like these:

A woman with flowing tresses that shawl her shoulders as she plucks a dulcimer. She is young, mature, her fingers delicate as a mother's tending to a newborn babe. Her face reflects an inner light. I see that the music comes from within her. The dulcimer is only a sounding board, an amplifier. There is a strange, haunting composition here. The woman, the instrument, are one piece, a painting with sound, a single entity, composed of separate elements that appear incongruous at first: wood, flesh, hair, smile, fingers, sound waves. I do not know the woman's name. I will love her always.

There are many of her here in these hills and hollows.

I saw her at folk festivals, on a downtown street in Branson, in a hardscrabble farm during the 30s. I saw her at the Globe Theatre in London, back in Shakespeare's time, in Yorkshire and Wales and Ireland. I saw her in Fayetteville and in the rugged hills of Newton County, Arkansas, somewhere in the smoke of Elkhorn Tavern and in the twilight along Osage Creek when the setting sun painted the water with all the colors reflected in her soft eyes.

The veins in Edna York's hands.

Michelangelo might have sculpted them. In her hands, I saw the road maps of pioneers who came from Compton County, Tennessee, settled in the Osage Valley in 1839. I saw the road from Bellefonte, through Capps, down to Fairview, the old name that has been wiped from the records.

Frank Stamps' face, another history of these hills, solid as the rock that houses his store in Osage, Arkansas. He is a man who offers friendship to strangers. He is a poem not yet

An Early Frost

written, a man of the earth and commerce, whose general store was better than any chain ever built. To him, a stranger is just someone he hasn't shaken hands with yet. He was the first Ozarker I ever met, and I credit him with making me want to stay when I didn't know where I wanted to go.

The following are just a composite of images that have left lasting impressions, but are not explained here. They are gestating, floating through my consciousness until they become transformed, indelible. Memories, after all, are shapeless, until fitted into context, made orderly, filed. But I want to mention these if only to spur me on to recall the wholeness of them at some later time. Put them more firmly into my mind's data bank.

Here they are, in collage:

Nameless people in campgrounds where I go, who brought me gifts they never realized I would cherish all my days. Their smiles, their interest, their love of the country. They told me of the best fishing spots, gave me directions to places off the tourist maps. They gave me their light, let me see into their good hearts.

Beauty

A girl in a bank; another in a newspaper office in Branson; a man in an auto parts store in Harrison; a teacher at Alpena; a chicken rancher down past Osage, near Huntsville; some reporters, newscasters; a fisherman who designs and makes lures, and retrieves them from the trees along Turkey Creek, near Hollister, Missouri; a stranger from Iowa I met on Lake Taneycomo; some of the York family who live near Alpena, Arkansas. Some women of talent who write novels that we will someday read and feel good about. A child swimming at the Blue Hole; a sunset that hung on forever one night over Table Rock Lake; a day at Silver Dollar City that took me back a hundred years in time, left me awestruck at what we have lost, proud of what we have preserved.

Charlotte, my wife, who planted our garden, worked long hours as a pioneer woman because the earth got under her fingernails and into her blood long after she was young and strong. Who followed me everywhere and who lived primitive beside me during the years of coming into these hills, becoming part of them in the only way you can: living with the earth, rather than just on it.

An Early Frost

Of course there are more of these memories. These are but a few that rose up in my mind, generating still other images of past and present times. I wander these Ozarks roads like a blind man, full of wonder at every turn of the road. This is being written in one of the campgrounds where I often go, some distance from my home. But the Ozarkers have given me lodging wherever I have gone; letting me hook up to their electricity, fish their ponds, hunt their woods, eat their simple foods.

There has never been a place like this on earth.

These feeble words are only a smattering of the heritage of these hills as seen by a grateful immigrant, a newcomer, an outlander.

This is but a glance at some of the beautiful things to be encountered along these endless Ozarks roads.

Look deep, see deep.

DRY COUNTY

His pickup jolts out of the yard like a P-40 bumping along an airfield in the South Pacific on a 1943 mission. It clears the junk and two of the coon dogs, grinds into second and sails over the entrails of a broken washing machine. Behind him, on the porch, his wife Alice stands disconsolate, a war-widow Greer Garson waving farewell to Walter Pidgeon. Only Alice is not waving goodbye. She is screaming at him in terror.

The truck skids in a tight turn, heading for the front gate, whining at the top of second gear. Old Ray's got the urge. The thirst. He's heading for Jasper to pick up a pint of moonshine. He ran out of beer at four o'clock that afternoon. He had trucked it all the way

An Early Frost

to Newton County, Arkansas, from Branson, Missouri, the day before. Newton County is dry, but Sunday is even drier--in both states. No time to run the border now. The risks are too great.

Never mind that Ray had one calf to doctor, some de- horning to do, and hay to set out on the lower pasture. With two six-packs of Old Milwaukee in his gut, he knew he'd never get across the creek, which was swollen from the recent rains.

Never mind that he'd promised Alice he wouldn't drink anymore. He'd tried to quit, Lord knows. Would have too, if it hadn't been for that other thing cropping up. He thought it was the arthritis at first, but the doctor said the bone was "plumb near gone near the elbow." Couldn't blame that on the drinking, either.

Sometimes the pain was so bad it brought tears to his eyes. Hell, the doc had given him a choice. But Ray didn't believe in doctors. Start operating on stuff like that it's liable to flare up and spread through the body a heap faster. Better to keep shut about it and try to kill the pain anyway you could. Of course the drinking was some worse now, but the only time the pain didn't matter was when he was stone drunk.

The pint jar had medicine in it. The only medicine Ray would take.

A lot of the men he knew were already there, sitting outside the pool hall when Ray banked his P-40 around the corner and jolted to a bucking stop in front of the Newton County Courthouse. He sat in his pickup for a moment, giving himself a quick debriefing. He lit a cigarette. It took him five paper matches to get it lit. He steadied himself. At 59, Ray took a minute or two to steady up from one of his three-day benders.

He opened the door and fell out of his truck. None of the men across the street said a word or made a sign. The light spilled over their backs like orange sherbet. They looked like men called back for a hundred–year reunion of the outfit, sad-eyed, wasted, frail, almost beyond hope themselves. They knew old Ray and his problem. They had known old Ray's dad, Jack, and his problem.

An Early Frost

Ray made it across the street, with a list to starboard. His red eyes caught the light and he looked away. The end of his cigarette is so sodden with saliva very little smoke gets into his lungs. He coughs anyway. A couple of the men nod to him. He nods back, with his whole body.

The pool hall is doing a little business. Mainly, the business is outside. Cars and pickups come and go. Men walk by, talk for a while, walk away. Quart and pint jars change hands. Sacks rattle. Money whispers. Grimy dollar bills move back and forth between palms, all wadded up or folded like packets of last wills and testaments.

Ray buys a pint jar of clear liquid. That's enough to get him through day three. He lurches back over to his pickup, leaning to port now. Before he gets in, he opens the jar and pours some 'shine down his throat. It burns all the way down. His eyes flash all the primary colors, in sequence. The cilia in his throat rebel at the sudden heat. He gags, but keeps the medicine down. He opens the door, begins looking for his keys. He looks all over for them; under the seat, on the seat, behind the seat. In all four pockets of his overalls. He takes another swallow from the jar. His hand spiders through the dust and mud on the floor of his truck. He sags into the seat, leans over the steering wheel, trying to think through pea soup fog clouding his brain. He bangs his palm into the ignition slot and lets out a cry. The keys are there. His palm has a thin indentation in its center.

Ray finishes the pint, but now he can't get out of the truck. He slides the window down, gulps for air. He fumbles some bills out of his pocket, sticks his hand outside and holds the bills up like winning tickets in a drawing. A bootlegger comes over to the truck with a sack. He shoves the sack in Ray's lap and takes the bills from Ray's hands.

"Better get on outa here now," the bootlegger says softly.

"Goin' on home," Ray says, using only a quarter of his mouth to speak.

He pats the sack, feels the pint jar inside. He belches and bile burns up into his throat.

An Early Frost

He felt bad about Alice, just then. He knew he ought to tell her, but he just couldn't. It was like saying he was no longer a man. He didn't mind her yelling at him about the drinking anymore. That way, she wouldn't notice the other thing, the way his elbow had shrunk and twisted out of shape. He wore long sleeved shirts and never let her see him without one on.

One thing, though. The cancer was slow. The pain pills hadn't helped much, so he'd given them up some time ago. He might last for years, he thought. Alice was taken care of, if he went. She could handle it if she didn't have to sit around and watch him go to pieces, literally. He didn't want her to baby him. She'd done enough of that. Ever since he'd come back from the war and married her. The farm was paid off now; plenty left for her to live out her days on.

He was suddenly tired. The way he got toward the end, flying the missions. Sometimes they had to drag him out of the cockpit, carrying him to the sack. He felt that way now. He knew he ought to get on home. He could get through it now, go on for another day. That was all he looked forward to now. Another day.

He twisted the key in the ignition. The truck jerked forward. He put in the clutch and twisted the key again. This time the motor roared to life, sounding just like his old P-40.

He put the shift lever into reverse, let out the clutch. The truck burned rubber in a tight turn.

Ray leaned out the window.

"Mission accomplished," he grinned. No one heard him, or if they had, none would know what he meant.

Ray's truck weaved away like a shot-splattered fighter plane. He had forgotten to turn on the lights. He headed for home, wounded.

He had fought the good fight.

Alice would be waiting for him, the runway lights on. Tomorrow, it will be Sunday. A day of rest.

A day of flags drooping at half mast.

UNTIL SHILOH COME

Jack Popejaw kept talking himself down into a deep black pit that day.

He had been in deep black pits before.

But none like this one.

The wine made it worse.

"I've had a bad week," he told himself. "High, low, jack and the game."

He sat on the front stoop of his trailer, an old mobile home that was rusting at the seams, its paint fading. It was one of those old silver 1945 government housing jobs that wound up as chicken coops or were stripped by some who made them into flatbed trailers. Jack's trailer was still alive because there wasn't a termite brave enough to get into the grimy, greasy, smokeflogged woodwork.

"Looky here, boy!" Jack shouted, shaking his thin, veined monkey fist at an imaginary figure. "You done turned into a monster."

He was talking to his son, Leonard, who was not there.

Leonard was nearly 17 years old.

"Smokin' 'at dope," said Popejaw. "That's what done us in. Dam' dope fiend."

Jack's mind raced like a ridgefire in the wind. Leonard, his son, was a dope fiend, all right; a monster. And Jack was going to do something about it as soon as he had swilled enough wine into his empty belly.

Wine gave Jack Popejaw the ability to think clearly, to see exactly who the enemy was.

The enemy, he determined, was a neighbor.

The neighbor was also a preacher-man. Not a regular minister or anything like that, but a self-styled California guru-type bearded hippie wearing a big smile, driving a big old car, and growing twelve-foot tall Tiajuana lettuce in his back yard.

The worst kind of neighbor, to Jack's rose-fogged mind.

Charles Sutterman, the neighbor, had come to Arkansas, bought the farm across the road from Popejaw. Jack was now convinced that Sutterman was selling dope to his kid. Leonard was over there all the time. And, when he wasn't over there, when he came home, he smoked dope. This made Jack angry. He was so angry most of the time that he got drunk at his son.

To teach Leonard a lesson.

That's what was happening this day. Jack was getting drunk at Leonard when the idea brightened in his mind that Charlie Sutterman was evil, perhaps Satan himself, and would have to be destroyed.

Jack had been drinking more than his usual dosage of wine that morning. And, too, Leonard was gone. Over at Sutterman's buying dope, Popejaw figured. The wine helped him to sort out these things.

Jack got to thinking about how Charlie had told the newspaper reporters about his mission in life. He said he worked with young people, trying to get them off drugs.

But, Jack knew better.

Charlie Sutterman was the devil, disguised as a preacher-man.

Oh yes. He was a dope dealer, and he was selling the vile weed to Leonard.

All of these things were clear to Jack this morning. They made perfect sense in his wine-soaked brain.

And, Popejaw got so drunk at Leonard that morning he experienced an epiphany. He saw all matters in the world very clearly. He attained an exalted state. He attained the status of a king, an oracle, all in the bleary twinkling of a myopic eye.

So, Jack broke open a new gallon bottle of wine.

"When you ride high, ride high," he said to himself.

He got his long-barreled goose gun out of the front closet. The shotgun was covered with dust. A spider had woven a web at the muzzle. He brushed it off, thought of his wife, Mary.

She was off working on a CETA program, sweeping the streets and gutters in the little town nearby.

Mary did this so that they would have food; so Jack could have his wine. When he drank, she thought he was very smart. He always told her what was wrong with the world and how to correct all its evils. He was good at this, but he only did it when he was wined up. So, she figured wine must be good for Jack. He told her it helped him to relax, relieved his painful rheumatiz', his "arthuritis." The wine, he told her, time and time again, was for his "stummick's sake" and, besides, "it didn't cost a whole heck of a lot for a poor man down on his luck."

Mary believed him, because she always brought home food stamps and always gave him enough from the CETA check so he could "make the run" to Berryville and buy his wine.

Jack loaded a #2 shotshell into the goose gun.

The gun was a single shot with a very long barrel.

"Geese," Jack always said, with a sly, gap-toothed smile, "need that kind of slick long barrel to get killed with."

Jack walked outside, his pockets rattling with #2 shells. He carried the jug of wine and the shotgun laid across the crook of his arm. He looked back at the mobile home, thought of the 13 acres he had there. Mary had made a small garden along the fence. The rest of the land was wild, overgrown with weeds. No matter. He paid $25 a month for rent. Rather, Mary did, with her CETA money she earned from pushing a broom down town streets on Highway 62 between Bear Creek and Berryville.

Jack headed across the road for Charlie Sutterman's modest farm. His eyes blurted out of their sockets like raw eggs streaked with red. His breath reeked of fermented grapes turned to alcohol.

He muttered private prayers that he made up in his muddled mind. Prayers of personal belief and power; prayers cribbed from scrabbled childhood memories when "granma" read from the good book. Jack sanctified his terrible mission in the private utterance of these half-remembered mutterings.

"I am Shiloh come," he said, without an inkling of what he meant, or what he heard from his own slick wine-shiny lips. It sounded right. It sounded righteous.

Charlie Sutterman was home. He looked out the front window, saw Jack Popejaw weaving toward his house, carrying the goose gun, the gallon bottle of wine.

An Early Frost

Jack saw Charlie, too, through the shadow-scrawled pane of his big city picture "winder," and his egg-eyes slid back in their sockets, as the hoods of his lids narrowed to canny slits.

"Evasive maneuvers," said Popejaw, ducking under the vast expanse of sky, slinking across the empty highway. He leaned to starboard because the goose gun was in his right hand. The jug of wine was in his left hand, for balance.

He weaved evasively over the asphalt, determined to sneak up on Sutterman and blow him to kingdom come--or to Hades.

Seconds later, he disappeared for a few minutes from Charlie Sutterman's view. There was a reason for this. Jack's feet took off on their own volition, careening him downslope, off the road's shoulder, into the ditch. He wallowed there, flailing his legs in the air like an overturned turtle, gasping for breath, humiliated.

When Jack managed to right himself and stand above the site of the ignominious fall, his lips and tongue were freshly crimsoned from a quick slug of wine sucked down his throat with all the aplomb of Popeye inhaling a can of spinach.

Popejaw, his spirit renewed, waved the long-barreled goose gun in the air (later, some would say "threateningly") and toddled, even more evasively than before, toward the house.

Leonard Popejaw was, in fact, within the Sutterman domicile. He was not smoking pot, but was actually "trying to get his head together" and explain the impossible: his father, Jack.

Charlie calmly ordered everyone in the house to run out the back door and hide in the field behind. He, too, ran out, when he heard Jack announce to the house, the sky and anyone within shouting distance, what he was going to do.

"I'm going to slay every one of you dope fiends!" Jack yelled. "I'm going to smite you, hip and thigh, with the jawbone of a Missouri mule, lay you low for selling my boy dope. I'm going to blow your heads off, you monsters! You're the devil, Charlie Sutterman, and you're going to burn in hellfire."

It was a strong speech for a man who never said much to anyone, either in kindness or friendliness, or in anger. Jack, perhaps, was a man who kept much inside himself.

Popejaw, following this brief, impassioned tirade, took a deep swig from his gallon jug.

"You in there, Charlie?"

No answer.

Jack swayed there like a dancer waiting for the drummer to start tapping his foot, for the band to strike up. The house seemed to stare back at him, its windows strangely like square eyes, the big picture pane empty, pained with silver and shadows left by the sun, black in vacancy.

Somehow, in the dim recesses of his befuddled mind, Jack knew the house had disgorged the enemy. A man living in the country knows the difference between an empty house and a full one. Charlie's house was plumb empty.

But, Charlie was somewhere around. Jack knew that, too.

"Sutterman, you som'bit," hollered Popejaw, "I kid you not. You done come to judgment day."

The empty house pulsed like a bellows, like something breathing.

Jack set the jug of wine down, raised the shotgun. The barrel swayed, as he tried to take aim at the house. The muzzle moved like a tracking device seeking a target. Jack tried to steady the long barrel, cranking his left elbow inward, underneath the stock, trying to keep his bent right arm at right angles to the weapon.

"Ah," he sighed, knowing he would never steady up. The muzzle swept past the front door like some heat-seeking device, wavered, swung back again. Jack sucked in his breath, squeezed the trigger, as the sight drifted toward the door once again.

The explosion rocked him on his heels. Fire spewed from the muzzle. A black cloud of lead bees spattered into the soft wood of the white frame house. Jack cracked open the breech and the empty hull shot out with a whoomping sound. He fumbled in his pocket for another shell. He shoved it into the barrel, excited now, and whacked the stock to close the breech with a brittle metalic clank of metal scraping against metal.

An Early Frost

   <u>Blam!</u>   He shot, reloaded, shot again.
<u>Blam!</u>
   Jack blammed out all the windowpanes. He
stalked the house, now, keenly intent on his
sacred obligation: to kill the house, the lair of
his nemesis, the enemy.
   Out of the corner of his eye, far off in the
back field, he saw the Sutterman kids sneaking
off through high, chigger-laden grass. He did
not see Charlie, Leonard, or Charlie's wife, Sue,
hugging the bank of the farm pond, their eyes
wide as brass buttons on a pair of Big Ben
overalls.
   Jack shot the house to death. He drank
more wine, shouted his divine rage to the
onlookers he could not see.
   The house looked abandoned, its broken
windows vacant and dark with jagged pieces of
glass making wounds in the empty frames.
   Finally, Jack walked up to the front door
and put the muzzle against the knob. He blew
a hole in the door's bellybutton and the blast
knocked him down. He got up, smiled, and
walked away, satisfied. He had used up his last
shell.

He walked back across the road to his own house. There, he stood in the front yard, among the dead hulks of rusted cars, the broken toys, the chicken droppings, and waited for the sheriffs to come.

He had not killed the preacherman, but he had destroyed the devil's temple. His work was done.

The sheriffs did come.

They surrounded Jack with popping flashes of lights atop white and maroon cars. They opened doors and slipped out to take cover behind the chicken house and the skeletons of oxidized automobile frames. They hid behind trees and the gaping doors of their jukebox-flickering machines. They came from two counties, and they meant business.

They drew pistols, leveled riot guns. At Jack.

He stood there with his goose gun, like a soldier-missionary on the field of battle. They didn't know he was out of shells.

"Hey there, Jack, why don't you put the gun down," one sheriff hollered. He was the local and knew Popejaw was a good old boy.

An Early Frost

"Why don't y'all go on back where you come from."

"Come on, Jack. We won't hurt you," said another sheriff, adding under his breath: "He ain't mean regular, but he looks plumb ready to kill anything big enough to die."

"Maybe he ain't real mean," joked a deputy, "but I don't see none of the mean ones a-messin' with him."

"What you got on your mind, Jack?" asked the head honcho, sheriff of the county.

"I'm gonna kill Charlie Sutterman for sellin' my boy dope."

"Let's talk about it."

"Ain't talkin' no more. I got to save my only son. I aim to wipe away all his sins."

"Come on, Jack. Put the gun down."

Jack swilled down a healthy swallow of wine. The goose gun swung a wide arc over a dozen men who ducked behind doors, car frames, a chicken coop, trees.

The bottle was empty. Jack tossed it at the nearest deputy. Someone cocked a hammer back.

"Aw," said Jack. He set the gun down, tilted his head back, looked straight up at the sky.

"Ain't nobody goin' to shoot you, Jack," soothed the head sheriff. "Get him, boys," he said, quietly, into his walkie-talkie.

The deputies moved, began to converge on Popejaw. They ran up, hunched over, running in military-like zigzag patterns. They looked, Jack thought, like a flock of fat, waddling ducks heading for the feed trough or the pond.

One sheriff picked up Jack's empty shotgun, cracked the breech open. He snorted. Another grabbed Jack's arm. Still another, shook him down, patted his clothes, dipped into his pockets.

Mary, Jack's wife, drove up a few minutes later, weeping. She rode in a highway trooper's car.

The head sheriff put handcuffs on Jack's wrists after jerking his hands behind the prisoner's back. Two men shoved Jack into the back seat of a sheriff's car. A young intense man slid in beside him.

Mary covered her wet face with trembling, praying hands. She was a thin woman, with a face and bone structure that might have attracted Modigliani. Jack's eyes flared as he looked at her, seconds before the sheriff's car drove him away.

"What's going to happen to my Jack?" she asked, disconsolately.

The state trooper sighed, his palm resting on the .357 magnum in his holster.

"He'll get a trial. He'll likely do time for malicious destruction of property. Better'n assault with a deadly weapon. The pros'cuter and his defense lawyer'll work out a deal. Nothing to worry about."

"What about that gun there?" she asked, pointing.

The trooper walked over, picked it up. He handed it to the local who knew Jack Popejaw, was, in fact, a cousin.

"We'll keep it, Mary. Don't you worry none. It's just a goose gun. No jury 'round here's gonna say this is a deadly weapon. Not in good old Jack's hands it ain't."

Mary looked at him through tear-stung eyes.

"What're you talking about, Mike?" she asked.

"Nobody wants to crucify Jack," he said.

Mary nodded, understanding. She looked across the road at the shot-out house, the one Jack had murdered. She looked at the empty wine bottle, at the yard, the sheepish lawmen starting to climb back in their cars. She resisted an urge to call to her son, Leonard, tell him to come back home. She turned, saw the grimy silver skin of the trailer shimmer bright in the afternoon sun. Her jawline tautened, turned hard.

"No," she murmured to herself, "nobody can't do that noway. He done it to himself a long time ago."

She turned, walked toward the old trailer that was home.

THE BOTTLE SHOP

The old man looked up at me from over bifocals that hung precariously from his nose. His wizened face seemed shrunk to his skull, the skin cracked with the dessicated rivulets of age lines, but his crystal blue eyes sparkled with youth. He wore a green eyeshade, faded purple shirt, elastic armbands on the sleeves, a vest that showed signs of moth larvae having fed on the cloth, and loose grey trousers that must have been cut from a fairly expensive bolt.

His shop bristled with a clutter of objects, artifacts, actually, that seemed more appropriate to the last century than this one. Certainly there was nothing in there of this presentera, yet the sign outside had not proclaimed the proprietor to be a dealer in antiques. In fact, the sign outside appeared quite modern, freshly painted in the last Branson vogue.

THE BOTTLE SHOP, it read.

Amos B. Abernathy, Prop.

The fogged windows had not allowed me to see inside. I had never seen the shop before, yet it was right on West Highway 76, crammed in between music shows and motels, go-cart rides and water slides. The other establishments were familiar to me, but not this one.

Curious, I went inside. The man seated at the ancient rolltop desk had to be Amos B. Abernathy. Good name. Uncommon in this day and age.

There wasn't a bottle in sight, oddly enough.

Just Abernathy, peering at me through those tiny lenses.

"Is this an antique shop?" I asked.

"No, sirree," said Abernathy, "everything's brand spanking new."

I looked around more carefully. Were these replicas? The items on sale did look new, yet they appeared to have been manufactured more than a hundred years ago. The brass shone, the wood gleamed, the pewter looked freshly cast.

Eccentric old coot, I thought.

An Early Frost

"Your sign says 'Bottle Shop.'"

"Yes, sirree, sir," cackled the old gentleman. "Right this way."

He stood up, and I noticed he was wearing spats. He had been writing in a ledger with a turkey quill pen. Puzzled, I followed him through a curtain to the back of the store. There seemed almost to be an atmospheric change between the two locations.

We seemed to step into a strange world of shifting light, wispy, uncertain colors, and a heady stream of exotic aromas.

There were shelves on the walls of the storeroom. These were lined with rows of various sized bottles filled with unknown substances.

"These are my bottles," said Abernathy. "Would you like to see what they contain?"

"They all seem to be filled."

"Indeed they are." The faint trace of a smile flickered at the corners of the old man's mouth.

"What's in them?" I asked.

He took a gallon bottle off the top shelf. The glass was clear and I could see a swirling mass inside. He handed it to me, somewhat gingerly.

I held it close and looked inside.

Clouds, small and full, floated in a blue sea miniature sky. It looked like the sky over Table Rock Lake. Mesmerized, I seemed to be able to smell the cedars and oaks, the fresh lake air, although the bottle was tightly closed.

"What is it?" I asked. "It looks like ...."

"Like the sky," he said. "Here's another." I set the first bottle down and took the other one from him.

The bottle was pure blue inside, flawless cobalt, but the mass seemed to be moving as though a wind were stirring within. Looking into its depths, I felt as though I was lying on a high treeless hill looking up at a summer sky. I looked at all of the other bottles. They were many-hued, orderly, beautiful in their neat rows on the shelves. Each one seemed to contain some different vision of the Ozarks sky. Now I could isolate the fragrances in the room. There was the faint scent of honeysuckle and morning glories, the smell of the lake before the sun has warmed its waters, the crisp aroma of roses, the winey scent of daffodils, the musty tang of deep woods cedars wafted on an after-noon breeze.

Fascinated, I looked at each bottle as the old man stood silently by, watching me.

There was one bottle with the ribbons of clouds colored gold by the setting sun. There was another with high thin altocumulus stretched all through the container. In still another, I saw silvery cirrocumulus lit by dazzling sunbeams. Each one seemed to contain a special part of our sky here in the Ozark hills, a miniature fragment of the heavens. A chill crept up my arm, the hairs on the back of my neck rose prickly as a spider's thread.

There was more.

Some bottles contained sections of a mighty river, whitecapped and frothy over the rapids, serene and motionless on wide bends. It seemed I saw wild trout leaping in one bottle, a flock of geese rise off the miniature surface of another. One bottle had what appeared to be a spring bubbling up from a deep cavern, spilling over flat stones into a woodland brook. My heart caught in my throat to see these wondrous, unexplainable things.

"I don't understand," I said, turning to the man at my side.

"Relics," he said. "For those who have forgotten what it's like to see blue sky, wild water and sun. Look at this one."

He handed me a bottle that radiated a pure bronze light at the very bottom, then turned the color of peach in the middle and shimmered golden at the top.

"Sunrise over the White River," he said. "The old White River, before it was dammed up, tamed."

"Incredible."

"These are very valuable bottles, my friend," said the man, his voice a serious rasp in his throat. "They are worth a great deal. In fact, they are as precious as life itself."

"You mean, these represent atmospheres that we no longer have on earth?"

"Yes. The pure air, the clean water, is all gone. This is the last place in the world where people can see the sky and taste the air. Do you understand?"

An Early Frost

"Yes," I said. "I think I do. It's been some time since I've been to the big cities, but it was very hard to breathe there. May I buy a bottle or two? For souvenirs?"

"Oh, no. They're not for sale, my friend. They're not for sale at all. You see, this is a museum; this bottle shop. This is where all of the beautiful vapors of this planet, the last airs and humours of life on earth are stored."

"But, it's not all gone. Not yet," I insisted. "Isn't it?"

He led me back out into the other room before I could say any more. He ushered me straight out the front door, back onto West Highway 76. I stepped into a sunny world that was every bit like a magnification of the substances inside the bottles.

Dazed, I walked to my car, got in. I drove to the park on Table Rock, near the dam, to the place where the pretty girls go in summer, where the boys bring their ghetto blasters and frisbees, where children fly kites and swim by the shore. The lake was dancing like a blue mirror. There was laughter. A few clouds floated cottony over the hills. The sky was a piercing cobalt.

The old geezer was crazy, I thought to myself.

Later, I drove back down West 76, stopped and parked the car. I looked for the sign that read "The Bottle Shop."

It wasn't there.

Instead, there was only a vacant building, ramshackle and weatherworn. I walked up and down the boulevard a long time before I gave up and went home.

It felt good to walk through our woods, to look out at Bull Shoals Lake from our back porch. The air was clean and fresh. The sky was clear.

What a wonderful time and place to be alive in, I thought.

It was good to breathe deep of the good air and to look up at the sky.

THE POACHERS

Parts of the following account are fantasy. Or, more properly, certain incidents fall into the category of "wish- fulfillment." The essentials of the material on poaching itself, however, are, unfortunately, true. I put this disclaimer in at the beginning for two reasons. One, I don't want to get a lot of letters from people who believe that every word I write is etched in truth. Two, it would be disconcerting, to say the least, if I were arrested, as if this document were an admission of guilt. Or a confession.

What are we talking about here?

Murder.

Cold-blooded, premeditated murder.

These were rough old boys. Spotlighting deer before the regular gun season opened.

The Poachers

They made pathways of light through the night-dark hills. Their beer breath wafted down the slopes, lingered faintly in the hollows.

The Ozarks are not pure.

Sure, most of the stills in this county, Carroll, have dried up, rusted away. Civilization has caught up with the moonshiners, too. Many of them are down to home brew and wild grape wine; toothless old men, full of memories, sit on creaking porches, heads cocked, as if listening for the sound of buckshot rattling through brush. Helicopters have replaced the Model T Ford. Grain has been replaced by clandestine gardens of cannabis sativa. Sour mash no longer bubbles in the fired iron pot deep in the woods. Grass, but not the kind you mow, is king. Northwest Arkansas' counties, and some parts of the Missouri Ozarks, resemble the Mexican state of Guerrero.

And, the word "guerrero," in Spanish, means "warrior."

This, then, is the setting.

The rough old boys drank beer and store-bought whiskey, however, instead of 'shine, when all this happened.

An Early Frost

They started out on the back roads in 4-wheelers about 3:30 a.m. Fifth of Ten High between the legs, half-pints of J.W. Dant in the big pockets of the G.I. jackets. Winchesters loaded, sighted-in at 100 yards. Skinning knives hanging on western belts embossed with flowers and names like Jack and Jim and Bill. Leers underneath bushy moustaches.

I found the doe gutted out, beheaded, haunches gone, steaks pried out of the carcass, mouth open in a silent scream, blue tongue lolling, eyes glassy and swarming with blue-bottle flies. Entrails scattered to the crows and turkey buzzards; a Jackson Pollack painting in relief. Thirty-ought-six hole in the neck, just below the spine. Lungs collapsed, rib cage twisted like an empty wooden crate.

The spike buck never had a chance. He had been dropped in the middle of the rough road just below the bluff. Long shot. Straight on. They must have gotten all of fifteen pounds of meat off of his tiny carcass. Poachers tend to hurry and it's hard butchering in the dark.

I waited for them the next night. I had heard them bragging at the old store that noon.

The Poachers

The four of them were responsible for the illegal killing of twenty-five to thirty deer per year. These boys kept clean tags until the last day of every hunting season. In the shadows of the store, with my Orange Crush, I listened to their campaign talk for the night ahead.

They were hunting over towards Bobo that night. Their Jeep moved fast. Lights bounced through the trees. Tires skidded over the rocky road. The air was rich with the smell of spilled bourbon and beer.

I caught them with their first kill steaming into the night. The fresh blood scent overpowered their own sweat- smell from booze-drenched pores.

The tracers helped.

The phosphorous and bullets zinged through the dark like incandescent bees. Sometimes it pays to save stuff from the war. Like training rounds.

They returned my fire, of course. I kept moving around, firing from behind thick oaks. Two of them ran toward the Jeep. For an instant, they were framed in the light from the headlamps. The tracers zipped into them. Smoke poured from their fallen bodies. I was careful not to shoot into the dry brush. I didn't want to cause a forest fire.

I hit another one in a bad place. He tried to run over the top of the hill behind the Jeep. He never made it.

The last man actually made it to the driver's seat. The tracers burned through the deer haunch in his arms. The stench of charred hair permeated the air. The man twisted into the steering wheel before he slumped into lifelessness, his wounds cauterized slightly by the burning phosphor.

Automatic weapons, thought illegal, are the choice in the matter of vigilantes versus poachers. The AR-15 converts easily to full auto. Night scopes, tracers that make beautiful, lethal scrawls in the air, help stack the odds against men who kill baby deer and sell the meat.

The archery deer season opened a day or so later. The woods were very quiet. I was hunting with a bow, wearing a camouflage suit. My face was streaked with camo paint.

I was almost invisible.

The Poachers

Yet, I had the odd feeling that someone was watching me.

THE GIRL DOWN THE ROAD

I always think of her standing on the porch waiting for me.

Of course, that's not the way it is, but I guess I try to fix her in my mind and hold her there for as long as I can and that's the way I have to do it.

When she stands on her front porch, she is very still. The sun is going down, making spectacular light plays in the green trees, the rays getting all tangled up and shooting out in different directions, burnishing the emerald leaves until you can't look at them anymore. Shadows lie all around the porch like the cast-off garments of children.

Girl Down the Road

She is staring down the lane, past the gate in the picket fence.

The sun is sliding down the edge of York mountain, but is stuck there for a long moment so that it catches her in a single dazzling beam. The fine loose hairs on her head are like spun fibers of coppery light, delicate as spider's silk. You wouldn't notice these usually if the sun wasn't stuck there on the corner of that mountain, wedged in there like a twenty-dollar gold piece. Her face is more distinct than it usually is. It is difficult to fix a face in your mind when you're too shy to look at it direct.

But, when she's standing there on the porch like that, bathed in light, caught there in the failing rays of the struck sun, you can see her features very clearly. You can see her eyes and the way the colors shift like the stone in a mood ring. Hazel eyes that pick up glints of gold from the sun and green from the leaves and bronze from her summer skin. The eyes are the hardest to hold in my mind. Even when she's standing still like that, her eyes are the biggest mystery about her. She is looking, but what does she see? What is she looking for, or who? Every time her eyes change color, I am puzzled.

An Early Frost

The first time I saw Hollie MacGuire, she was picking berries at the old, abandoned, Griffin place. There had been nobody living there for years, but the blackberries didn't know that--they grew in wild profusion all over the meadows and the hills.

Hollie was singing some little song to herself. I couldn't hear the words, but her voice was musical, soft. I always cut through the Griffin place to go down to where the beaver have built dams on Osage Creek and pooled up the water over deep holes where the smallmouth bass lurk in their secret underwater nooks. I was carrying my fishing pole and a plastic box full of lures, a knapsack with a sandwich and a couple of colas in it.

I made a noise and Hollie stood up in the blackberry thicket, startled.

Her lips were purpled from nibbling on berries. But the sun caught her hair and spun through it, threading it with golden honey. She smiled at me after a frowning moment and something inside me melted. She blew a strand of hair away from her mouth. The simple dress she wore was faded from many washings. She was thin, with a frail, country-girl strength in her bones and limbs. She seemed full of a sad joy that I can't explain. As if she had found something wonderful that was too late to enjoy as she once might have, like discovering a favorite childhood doll in an attic trunk that stirred up memories of other times.

"You're the man who lives down the road," she said.

"Yes. Jim. Jim Lawrence."

She told me her name.

"You must be Pat MacGuire's daughter. He plowed my garden for me this spring."

"His wife," she said, a shadow sliding across her face.

MacGuire was in his sixties. This was no more than a girl. Nineteen? Twenty? She looked even younger than that. Well, this was the Ozarks. Such things happened, I was told.

She looked at me oddly. I was staring. My mouth dropped open.

"I'm sorry. You look so young," I stammered.

"I'm eighteen."

"Yes." I didn't want to say any more. My mouth tasted of foot as it was.

An Early Frost

"Want some berries?" She held out her pail to me. I took one, more to be close to her than anything else. She smelled of the fragrance of earth and growing things. There were scratches on her arms from the brambles, white streaks on suntanned skin. Her hair was tied back with a faded ribbon, but the loose strands kept moving over her face, as if caressing her. Her eyes were large, bright. Open, like her face. A book to be read, studied.

"Going fishing?"

I nodded.

"Can I watch?"

I guess I shrugged. It's hard to remember now. She came with me down the path to the beaver dams. I found a spot, put on a yellow #2 spinner, snaked it along between the bank and a beaver house. The second cast brought a bass out of hiding. I felt the line pull taut and then the water boiled.

"Oh!" she exclaimed. "You got him. Big one!"

She laughed like a child as I played the bass, reeled him in. I threw him on the bank and the sunlight smelted silver on his sleek skin, stippled it with pastel colors of the rainbow. I took him out of the grass and slid a stringer through a gill. I secured one end of the line to a strong root sticking out of the bank, tossed the fish back in the water.

"I love fish," she told me. "Pat doesn't fish much anymore. He used to take me fishing up at Table Rock."

I caught two more smallmouths, a sunfish, a big bluegill and a sucker. I threw the sucker back in.

"I'd like you to take the fish," I told her, "cook them up for you and your husband." The last word was a lump of cornmeal dough in my throat.

"Oh, I couldn't do that."

"Sure. I can't eat all these. No freezer. But I fish all the time. Take them."

"Thank you, Jim."

I took the lure from my swivel, put it back in its plastic box, fastened the swivel to an eye on the pole. I sat beside her in the shade.

"I'll split my sandwich with you," I said, pulling it from my pocket. The sandwich was bent. Hollie laughed and it sounded so strange

An Early Frost

I wondered if it had been a long time since she had laughed like that.

I smoothed out the crumpled sandwich, took it from the plastic sack and pulled it into two pieces. She took her half with its ragged edge when I handed it to her.

She ate without self-consciousness. When we were finished, I leaned back against the tree and watched Hollie take the hem of her dress and dab off the corners of her mouth.

I wanted to know about her.

"Have you been married to Pat very long?"

"A year. We been married a year now. Almost. Are you married?"

"Not anymore." I didn't want to tell her about it, but she leaned forward, her legs drawn up in a bipod, her arms folded across her knees. "Divorced." I didn't tell her that my wife had broken me in half, that she had brought another man in to our home when I was on tour with an exhibition of my paintings. I couldn't tell her that I had lain broken and fallow for a year until I had left Colorado and come to the Ozarks just to try and find myself again. I had not been painting very much, but I was healing.

Girl Down the Road

I didn't know much about Pat MacGuire. He had been neighborly. For six months, I'd been hacking out a place to live, on ten acres I'd bought from an estate. My house was small, comfortable.

"Mr. MacGuire took me to his home--after my folks-- died," she said, in answer to my question about the taciturn man who had plowed my garden. "He thought he ought to have married me, so he did. He--he's nice to me."

"What happened to your folks?"

Hollie looked down at her feet. She wore sneakers that were worn at the toes. No socks.

"They were killed. Mr. MacGuire's son did it. He's in prison now. His name was Wilbur. He robbed them and killed them with a gun 'bout five years ago. They used to own the store up on the highway. They didn't have much money, but Willie thought they did. He got a .22 pistol and shot them to death one night. Mr. MacGuire, he took me in, and then when I got grown, he thought we maybe better get married. Wasn't his fault his son was bad. He took some of the blame, I guess."

An Early Frost

The lump in my throat wouldn't go away. I had heard the story, of course. It had been so distant from me then, but now I would remember it every time I went by that little store up the road.

"I'm sorry," I said.

"It's all right. It happened some time ago." I started tearing off blades of grass to put in the plastic sack where I would put the fish she would take home. I'd fill the sack with creek water to keep them fresh.

I wanted to ask her more about Pat MacGuire, but I didn't trust myself.

"How come you moved out here?" she asked me, as I was taking the fish off the string.

"There was a gallery over by Eureka Springs that showed my paintings. They told me about the country here. I just wanted a place that was quiet, secluded. So I could paint."

"Mr. MacGuire said you was a painter. What do you paint?"

"People. Places."

"I'd like to see them sometime."

"Okay." I wanted her to see them right away. I wanted to sit her down in the room I was making into a studio and start sketching her face, searching for that elusive core beneath the surface that would reveal her inner life. I wanted to just look at her and listen to her talk. In her speech I heard music, rippling guitars, dulcimers, keening rivers and the wind whicking over stones and whispering through hay fields, rustling in graceful stands of corn.

"I have to get back now," she said, getting up. "Mr. MacGuire will want his supper. I'll cook the fish, make berry muffins. I'd ask you over, but it's not my place to offer."

"I understand," I said. I didn't want her to go. For a moment she stood there and I thought it would be easy to just kiss her. I handed her the sack of fish, pulled the knapsack over my shoulder.

We said goodbye on the road.

She waved again when she turned up the lane to her place. She held up the plastic sack of fish for me to see. Impulsively, I blew her a kiss. It seemed to me that she stiffened for a moment, but I could be wrong. It might have been a trick of the light, although I had trained myself to notice such things. I was a fair painter.

An Early Frost

I went back through the Griffin field many times after that. I never saw Hollie picking berries again. I saw only crows, blackbirds, jays. A rabbit or two. Once, a covey of quail burst from the berry thicket and the silence afterwards reminded me of her somehow.

One evening, I strolled over to see Pat MacGuire. Hollie was standing on the porch, looking down the lane. I watched her for a long time as I unlatched the gate and walked up to the house. Before I got there, however, she went inside. Pat came out and talked to me. He was polite, gruff. His pipe tobacco smelled stale, old. He never invited me in. He thanked me for the fish I had given Hollie some three months before. He said he'd like to go fishing with me sometime.

"This is from my garden, Pat." I handed him a sack of zucchini, bell peppers and tomatoes grown from ground he had plowed. He took the sack and thanked me. Debt paid.

When I got to the gate, I looked back. The porch was deserted.

I never saw Hollie again. But I always think of her as standing on that porch, waiting for me. Maybe I'm reading it all wrong, but that's what I think. I have already painted her standing on that porch, just before dusk settles on the land. I stare at the painting and wonder if it will come alive. I stare at the images there and see Hollie, standing there, waiting for me.

She is all alone in the portrait. Just waiting.

Waiting.

AFTER QUAIL

Early morning. Arkansas. Just south of Alpena. It's quiet, like a battlefield just before the guns open up. Just before the men move into their fighting positions.

Eerie out there on the road. We come to the barbed wire.

We pull the wire hoop off the post and open the gate. Duke, the German short-haired bird dog has already crawled under the fence, leaving behind tufts of his hair, like trout flies, grey and brown hackles stuck to the barbs.

We close the gate together. Then we jack shells into our shotguns. The morning sun spills through the trees, into the field, like running honey.

Quail

My friend Dennis and I put some short yardage between us, stalk toward the gully, flow into it. It is overgrown, thick with cover. Looks good. We talk with our eyes, watch Duke as he sniffs the grass. The dew has been mostly burned off, but underneath, the gouts hold scent. We take hunters' positions. Our shotguns gleam dark blue in the sun. We wear camouflage outfits, shooting vests.

We might have been Special Forces troops on patrol, sneaking through the jungles of Nam, or wading up a ravine in Korea that looks amazingly like Camp Pendleton, California.

Shotgun shells weigh down our vests. Duke sniffs the ground ahead, ranges wide, like a wind-up toy, tail high, flickering. Quick as a ferret, he drifts far out, then back in, following invisible lines through the sheared remnants of alfalfa.

We walk on a path, come to a clump of weeds and denuded berry tangles. Duke goes to point. He hunches forward, lifts his right paw, cocks it backward, nose into the brush.

On point, Duke is rigid, a tan and white sculpture anchored to the earth. His tail is cocked high, his body slanted forward like some eternal 3-D photograph.

We circle the brush, shotguns at the ready, safeties eased off. Behind me, the rest of the squad waits, M-16s oiled and gleaming, nervous stomachs rippling with grey masses of churned food and gas, intestines taut, slippery coils smoking with gases in dark abdominal caverns. The patrol is fanned out slightly, the men's faces smudged with camo paint, black and olive and green smears that wipe out their identities.

The thicket produces no birds. We encircle it, infiltrate it, stomp it impatiently. Duke sniffs out a new trail, disappears in the brush. We become ourselves again, just a pair of hunters out to bag some quail during the waning days of the season.

A few minutes later, Duke goes into a point again. His tail juts high, crooks slightly into the bent arrow of a weather vane. His right foot cocks backward. A class hunting dog pose. Currier & Ives, Field & Stream, Outdoor Life.

Dennis and I step forward, flank the dog.

Quail

"Easy, Duke," says Dennis as the dog begins to lean forward, his coat rippling over bone and muscle.

Quail burst out of the thicket in a rattle of fluttering wings. They sound like stirred-up rattlesnakes. Dennis' 20- gauge double barrel coughs once. A bird crumples in mid-air. I sweep the 12-gauge pump over a bird's silhouette, spray him out of the air with a squeeze of the trigger. I pump a new shell into the chamber, angle on another bird. Too late, too far, but I fire anyway, caught up in the thrill of the moment.

Dennis picks up my bird. He can't find his. Duke points it, but the quail is invisible on the ground. Finally, Dennis reaches down, picks up the dead bird, drops it into a jacket pocket.

The hills roll on before us. Duke ranges in a circle. We step after him to pick up the singles.

It is a long morning, full of blood and smoke and feathers. It is a twenty-mile day and my forty-odd years drop from my shoulders like layers of shed skin. My cocker- spaniel, Lady Kay, dead for more than twenty-five of those years, barks down the long halls of my memory.

An Early Frost

But, that was back in Colorado, and there are no pheasants here in this northwest corner of Arkansas. There are no fields of wheat-stubble stretching to the foothills of the Rocky Mountains.

There are just barely audible whispers of these old forgotten things as Duke pauses before another thicket pointing at birds we cannot see.

The silence, just before we flush the quail, is full of these whispers, a distance sussurance heard only in the mind.

The boom of shotguns, feathers flying from shot quail, floating down to earth. This time, the quail stay up a long time, the singles scattering wide, zooming clear to the bordering woods.

We cross the ends of the earth tracking down the singles.

A young brown face pops up beyond the rusted tangle of concertina wire. I cover his face with the muzzle of my M-1 carbine, take him out with a short squeeze of the trigger. He falls in the Korean ditch like a broken wing, lies there like a doll. Something clawed grabs my stomach. Something tightens around my chest, shutting off my breathing.

Sweat drips into my eyes. My vision blurs. I see everything through a petroleumed camera lens, everything in soft focus.

Dennis stops, looks back at me. He looks very young. He is young.

"You all right?" Soft Arkansas drawl.

I look around. It's late morning on the Williams farm. Plenty of game cover here. Fence rows. Thick clumps of brush in the gullies. We move in, Dennis and I, at angles.

I wipe thick sweat from my forehead.

We wear the morning away, break for lunch under a shady oak. Duke gets his share of sandwich.

Late in the day, we are still hunting. A single jumps in front of us, peels off like a fighter plane. Dennis swings on the whirring bird. Parooms a shot. Behind a foot. The quail jerks, corrects its course. I clock him, swinging from behind, as he passes at the near end of my range, blot him out in the sight picture, keep swinging on past him at the same speed, squeeze the trigger while the barrel is in motion. I dump him out of space with thwacks of shot that shear off a pinch of feathers. Caught him right at the tail end of the string, 40 yards away, with number 7 chilled shot.

We picked up two more singles, got into another covey. Four birds dropped out of that one. There was a whirring in my ears all the way home to Osage in Dennis' pickup. I thought back on the day.

I've got almost twenty years on Dennis. He's a fine shot, doesn't talk much. A good hunting partner in my book. He was polite enough not to ask me about a couple of episodes I had out there. He didn't say anything about the sweating, the times I drifted off, back to Lady Kay and the Colorado wheat fields, back to Korea on patrol, back to ....

Hunting with my father. I had blocked that out. But, it was there. I had sons, some not much younger than Dennis. I had never hunted with them, not pheasants, not quail, not dove, deer. I missed my father, and maybe I missed what I never had with my oldest sons, that rare companionship you find out in the field, under the sky, in the woods.

"You shot well today," Dennis said. "Real good."

"You too." I almost called him "son."

"I missed that last one," he laughed. "Way behind him."

"A few inches."

"You got him. Clean and nice."

"He flew right into it. The Remington throws a good pattern at forty yards."

"Yah, it does."

I remembered something Dennis had told me earlier.

His father had never hunted with him as my father had hunted with me.

"Want to go again?" he asked, when we pulled up at my place.

"Anytime, son. Anytime."

GRANNY: A LOVE STORY

I met Granny a few months after we moved to Arkansas. She was a pioneer and had lived in the Ozarks for over eight decades. Now, she is gone.

Granny had an insidious growth in her body that they call oat-cell cancer. I don't know what this is, but it's very tiny and very destructive. It was draining the light from her eyes, thinning her sinews, and spreading pain through her frail body.

The first time she held out her small hand and cracked a worn smile, I fell in love with her. She was right at home in her rocking chair on the front porch. There were no modern conveniences in her home. And, she had the kind of home that was somewhere near you, near us all.

Granny

The house had not been painted in years. The boards were weathered to a silvery grey, and the hand-froed shingles had been patched with cedar over the years. Inside, she cooked over an old wood stove. There always seemed to be a few glowing coals in the firebox, the lingering smells of fresh-baked bread or stewed squirrel, bluegills fried in cornmeal batter. The living room was small, cozy. A potbellied stove sat in its center so that the room was democratically warmed. She had a battery-operated radio so that she could listen to church services and Grand Ol' Opry. On the front porch, there was a butane-powered refrigerator. These were the only modern touches to a home lit by lamplight, graced with religious prints on the walls, samplers in old frames.

She remembered the old days with a fine mind full of memories. She reflected on her past with clarity and affection despite the bitter years of drouth and economic depression. When she spoke, it was like listening to a brook rippling over stones. Her voice rasped with half-whispered memories, as if she was speaking from the past itself.

An Early Frost

She talked of her children, her husband, buried not far from her house, in a cemetery grove lined with massive oaks that shaded the stones, the mounds long since sunken into the loamy earth. There was no dejection in her talk, no rancor.

She had seen life and she had lived it. She knew what the gone days meant, what hardships she had been through and that suffering was often a part of it. Now, she could sit on her porch and look down through the pasture and past the far gate and see way beyond the place where she would live out her last days. Way beyond.

A surviving son lived with her, one of seven or eight children, a man who had been crippled by polio, but had grown up like a weather-gnarled tree, defiant of his apparent handicap. Red, as he's called, planted their garden, raised the chickens, took care of the two dogs and calf, the 40- year-old mule named Pete. He hunted the game that was part of their diet, and cut their firewood. Under Granny's careful scrutiny, of course. Red was a twin. His brother had died several years before, leaving his shadow in the earth around the old place, in the faded photographs Granny showed me one day.

Granny used to give us fresh milk. If it was going bad, she said that it was turning "blinky." She and Red would skim off the cream to make their butter, but the milk was still very rich. She gave us seeds, as well, in little handfuls, or the vegetables themselves, from which we could extract the seeds and dry them for next year's planting. She gave us a huge cucumber once, telling us to wait until it "swiveled up." We did as she said and planted those seeds one spring. When we ate the cucumbers that grew from the seeds in that "swiveled up" cucumber, they were very sweet to the taste.

Some days Granny wasn't always up to snuff. When I asked her how she felt, however, she would always answer, "tolable well." I knew she was sick. Still, the smile was there, sometimes forced so much that it hurt both of us.

There is a spring branch that runs through Granny's place. Sometimes it runs full and rampant over the shale ledges and sometimes it slows to an almost silent seep over the rocks.

An Early Frost

The water keeps running, though, as it has for many years. Granny commented on it often, took pleasure in its energy. It was a life-giving source for her and Red, and she never failed to give it homage. She was proud of the water and there was always a pitcher full to pour for guests.

Granny has passed on now, but the branch still flows. Now, as I write this, I want to go to her porch once again and look out at that branch, think of her. I want to see it keep running forever now that she's gone. I want to see it smile as it passes by Granny's old house on the way to Osage Creek, to the Blue Hole where the children swim. I want to see it smile as it did when she was alive, a reflection, somehow, of her indomitable spirit. For I know what that is out there, shining through the trees, full of sunshine and warmth. Not just a stream bubbling up out of a hidden spring deep in the rocky earth. Not just a trickle of water where deer and quail and squirrel drink, but a smile.

Granny's smile.

COYOTE

A grey shape moving out of grey sleep, he stalks the nightland of the Ozarks like a phantom created out of mist. He pads over the hills like the night itself, dark in dark places, moonlit in moonlit spaces, blending into the chiaroscuro of hollows, whispering over the ridgecrests with an easy loping gait, part of the hills, part of the silence, part of the death that inhabits the lonesome stretches of woods.

This is the coyote, a denizen of these rolling hills, seldom seen, always there, hunting, prowling the outer edges of civilization, brother and outcast, pariah and neighbor. I have heard him moving in packs, belling like some lost hound of hell as he wanders the vast Ozarks in search of prey.

An Early Frost

Some call him a scavenger; some say he's a predator. Still others say he's brother to the wolf and a needed hunter to cull the sick and the lame animals from the land. He's resourceful and wears many guises. He does hunt the slower deer, and he can outwit the rabbit and the squirrel. He will take what he finds, for hunger is a thing his belly knows all year long.

I've seen him use his comely females as bait to lure an unsuspecting male dog into the woods where the pack can tear him to shreds. I've seen him bested in a fair fight with a raccoon and I've seen him run from a deer in the velvet like a scared pup. I've seen him smile and I've seen him kill.

The coyote is a changeling, a chameleon in fur. He is ubiquitous, like the wind that scurries in dark places. He is as elusive as the whippoorwill, a shadow that runs on four padded feet, a pair of eyes that peers from a thicket in the Mark Twain National Forest, along the Current at dusk, down on Opal Wake's farm near Osage, Arkansas, in the hollow where the creek runs below our home on Bull Shoals Lake.

In his various disguises, the coyote is a rollicking puppy, a cold-blooded killer, a frightened cur with its tail tucked between its legs, a wistful reminder that the dearest and gentlest house pet has the vestigial heart of the hunter, more than a few droplets of savage blood humming in its veins.

The coyote is a survivor.

He has been tracked, trapped, hunted, shot, poisoned, slaughtered, in a hundred different ways. He has been called cattle-killer, sheep-slayer, feeder on carrion. He has weathered the epithets and the cyanide bullets, the steel traps and the strychnine. He has remained free, despite man's passion to annihilate his species, and kept his territory clean. He has maintained his precarious balance during an ecological nightmare.

Mister Coyote may, in fact, survive us all.

While he steps out of his role of balancing the wildlife population occasionally, he is essentially a needed creature (as all creatures are), one who keeps the deer herds healthy and down to size so that starvation and disease do not stalk the land in his place. He is the doctor, the shepherd, the thankless conservationist.

Man has detested the coyote, has tried to eliminate him, has chased him to the ends of the earth. Man has treated him with contempt, with disdain, and sometimes, with ignorance of his true value. But the lowly coyote is worthy of man's respect, despite the times he has given the farmer, the rancher, the shepherd, just cause for concern.

He is neither the lowliest nor the most exalted of God's creatures. He is, for the most part, a diversified creature in an age of specialization. He is not the enemy we have too often thought he was, despite his secretive, anti-social ways. This enigma of the canine world is the subject of ancient Indian myths and stories, the anti-hero of modern day cartoons.

He is still a part of the Ozarks, still a part of our own myths.

Despite his many masks, the coyote may be a friend to man, after all. If, one day, he is put on the list of endangered species, we may find ourselves on the same sad and tragic list.

ONCE UPON A FARM

There was once a fine farm on a road, with a hill behind it, and a field in front of it that sloped gentle toward a lazy creek full of fish and crawdads, beaver and mink, water spiders and the chipped flint arrowheads left behind by summering Indians who lived off the land and left almost nothing behind to memorialize their existence.

The farm was built long after the Indians had been driven off the land, crushed out of existence, absorbed into the blood of a people crazed on the concept of "Manifest Destiny."

The farm was modest, small in acreage, but tucked back away from the main roads so that the man who built it, worked it, could live peaceable and Christian, according to his heart.

An Early Frost

The farmer's name was Jethro Gibson, and he had come to the Ozarks from the hills of Tennessee. He lived there on his farm for many years, grew a family, saw his children move away, far away to California, saw his wife's health deteriorate, his garden shrink, his fields go fallow and weed over. Everyone thought Mrs. Gibson would die first. But, that was not to be.

I think old Jethro collapsed in the shed next to his garage. Died of a heart attack. A neighbor, Elwyn Newshire, found Mr. Gibson there, tried to help him. Elwyn is a polio victim and doesn't have full use of his arms and legs. He manages, though. Mr. Gibson didn't survive, however. There were two little houses on the place, besides the garage and shed. One of the Newshire women lived in one house for a while, taking care of Mrs. Gibson. Then, Mrs. Gibson passed on, as they say out here in the Ozarks.

The Gibson place is out of the way. It's around twenty- five or thirty miles to the nearest large town. There is a little country store out this way, about three or four miles distant. You can get a lot of things at that little store and the prices are about the same as you would pay in the Berryville, Green Forest or Harrison markets. I don't know how he does it.

Anyway, there's no one there at the Gibson place anymore. In fact, Elwyn and his mother, Edna, don't live next door, either. She has passed on, Elwyn has moved to a small town.

The Gibson place has never been for sale. I asked why and somebody told me the family just kept it for sentimental reasons. There are two old cars there, rusting away. One is a Ford, the other a Mercury. They were intact when we moved in here, about a mile from there. Since then, they've been stripped, gutted, the windshields blasted away by shotguns. The clear glass is now opaque, a complex of shattered crystals more intricate than a spider's web.

The gravelly country road, tire-lethal with flint chips, runs right through the abandoned farm. The branch runs below the garage and shed, into Osage Creek. On the other side of the road are the two small houses. Side by side. Their windows stare broken and vacant onto the road. The mailbox is a nesting place for rats. So is the shed and garage. The houses are nesting places for everything: wasps, snakes, rabbits, owls, mice, rats, and immortal cockroaches.

There are things in the houses. I've seen some of them. But, going into the old houses is sad. There are always pieces of clothing that belonged to the children, or to the parents who died after the children left home. There are the cupboards with a few items of food still left on the shelves, the labels faded, the cans swollen from poisonous gases, the ragged cardboard remnants of boxes almost fossilized after being chewed up and used for nests or privys by small animals. Heaped up rodent droppings make a miniature landscape atop the rotted linoleum.

The things are: a cook stove, some beds, calendars and newspapers, broken cups, a religious scene hung in a frame on the wall, some pieces of toys, parts of a wood heating stove, rags, a few dirty drinking glasses on the warped drainboard next to the stained sink. There are some susurrous shadows in the rooms that don't belong to anyone anymore. They were just left there like worn out longjohns to keep company with the dust and move around with the sunlight that manages to get through the dirt-caked windows. There are, too, some old sad echoes that are so faint you have to strain to hear them: "Pa, supper's on the table; give me the doll; here comes the mailman; now, you fetch that milk; goodbye, Mom; they's a copperhead under the porch; looks like rain."

There are a couple of apple trees in the front yard. We went there, my wife and I, one day to get the apples. We had been watching the trees for a long time, waiting for the fruit to ripen. There was no reason to let those apples go to waste. When they started to fall, we went down the road to the Gibson place the next day to pick the apples. It was time. In fact, it was just past time.

When we drove up, the trees were full of blackbirds and crows. They perched on the branches in a drunken stupor, gorged on ripe apples.

Every apple on the trees was gone. Eaten up by the birds. Of course, there's no telling how long those birds had been coming to the Gibson place to eat ripe apples. Or overripe apples. Some of the apples must have fermented, turned their juices to a kind of simple wine.

Behind the place, up a steep hill, on a level, there were berry bushes, thick, tangly. And, near the creek there was another field full of blackberries. One summer we watched these ripen. We walked there every day to be sure the birds didn't beat us to the harvest. The vines were sagging with luscious ripe blackberries. The vines were so thick you would have had to chop a path through them with a machete.

The day came when we got our tin buckets and walked down the road to the Gibson place to pick blackberries. Our buckets gleamed silver in the sun. It was a glorious morning. We came to the field. There wasn't a berry bush in sight. Someone, we never found out who, had come by and brushhogged the whole field. I guess they must have chopped them down and loaded them up in a truck. We asked around and none of our neighbors knew anything about it. What was once a field full of berry bushes was only an empty chopped field. We looked up at the two houses and behind them. The brushhoggers had been there, too. The ground was as clean as a hen's egg.

We scrambled up the hill to the level behind the empty houses. Berries were hard to find, but we found some. Our buckets weren't full, but we had enough to show for our efforts. There weren't enough for a pie, but enough for a sprinkling on our cereal the next morning.

There just isn't anything to pick there anymore. Between the birds and the bushhoggers, there just isn't any use trying to get something for free. The wild winged creatures know the right day to come. We're always a day late.

I used to hunt quail back of the Gibson place. And rabbits. One young man I know sometimes sits up in a tree and watches for the deer to cross the upper field.

We saw a wild turkey hen there one day. She was beautiful, very regal. Now, though, I don't even see any game there on autumn afternoons. Once my dog got stuck under the garage and it took me almost an hour to free him. He had been hunting with me and he disappeared. I was walking down the road when I heard his pitiful cries. It took me ten minutes to find out where he was. He had gone inside the garage and fallen through some rotted boards. I had to take out part of a sideboard to pull him out of his trap. He won't go near the place now.

There are a lot of abandoned farms down this way. I think they call them hard-scrabble farms. People die. They move away. They never come back. Everything just falls apart. Nobody seems to want these farms. Maybe they're jinxed, like the Gibson place seems to be. I don't know. I still go over there once in a while. I stand out there on the road by the mailbox that's a nest for rats and look at the houses, the workshed, the garage, the two old cars.

It's very peaceful there and I can imagine how it must have been once. If I close my eyes for a moment, I can hear the people laughing and talking. I can hear Bob White piping on the hill, see the deer nibbling the apples. I can hear someone calling me to supper and I can smell the aroma of blackberry pie cooling, sweet and sassy, on the summer window sill.

HOT AUGUST RAIN

It's hotter than the hinges of hell in the Ozarks.

Even the oak leaves sweat; the dankness boils out of the earth, drenches the ticks, smothering them with moisture.

August opens up like a blast furnace, curdles the blood, welds the mind shut, blots the eyes with the blinding salt of perspiration. The sun hammers the graceful stalks of corn, wilting green leaves, burns through to the heart of tomatoes, squash, cool melons sleep-growing under shady vines; stirs up violent insects, the big, bloodsucking shiny-bodied flies, the mosquitoes, the gnats, setting them to swarm in the humid air like a pestilence, like an ancient

An Early Frost

vengeance set upon the summer land for no good reason.

The candy-apple painted motorcycle roars through Lampe, Missouri, on a rampage.

It leaves its black tracks on asphalt and its smoke hanging in the air long after its twin tailpipes disappear from sight, like the vacant dark eyes of snakes sliding back into dark cool thicket.

You can smell oil and leather, vinyl and chrome, rubber and gasoline, for five minutes after the red machine passes. The crackle of its engine whine lingers in the ears like the nattering whine of a mammal-seeking mosquito.

Kimberling City. A small boy smacks his lips at the motorcycle's passing. A teenage girl, in shorts and halter, halfway to the ice cream parlor, takes a deep breath and feels the wind in her hair, dreams of faraway places, freedom, the alluring roads where the iron horse is master. She tries to glimpse the rider, a faceless youngster in a full helmet, cutoff T-shirt clinging to tanned skin, looking like a knight on a fast steed, but he whips by her like an old memory from a book about King Arthur. She thinks he is beautiful, and a deep, primordial longing rises in her heart like a song.

An old man at the service station where Highway 13 and West 76 come together, whistles to himself as the Honda streaks by, banks for the turn, the rider part of the machine, the machine part of the rider. He thinks of his old Harley flathead buried in a barn up in Christian County, its rust now part of the earth, its chain slack and silent.

Another man, across the way, gets into his car, mutters under his breath. His eyes porcine with a dull hatred. Motorcycles. He hates them blindly because they are there, all over the country and they annoy him. He can never see them on the road, and they are always passing him, weaving in and out of long lines of cars when he is stuck behind the flat back end of an 18-wheeler in 90-degree heat. He starts his Buick with an angry twist of the key in the ignition and exults in the roar of his powerful engine. He drives out of the service station, aiming his car like a shark at some unseen swimmer beyond his vision.

A tourist, a widow who worked as a librarian and was once a member of a prominent sorority, watches the young rider hurtle past her, and she senses his speed, his daring, the cool courage he shows as an earthbound mortal wishing to fly like an eagle. Her husband had been a crop duster, his blood surging with speed and beer, his body smelling of petroleum. She recalls her husband now, as the acrid smoke from the bike curls at the flares of her nostrils.

Her husband had ridden an ancient Indian, but he had died of pneumonia in a local hospital long after the chemicals had ruined his lungs from ten years of spraying dust and death over fields far to the south where the cotton and the rice grow in Arkansas valleys.

She hates the motorcyclist, too, for her own private reasons.

Past Lakeview, past Silver Dollar City, past Shepherd of the Hills, the sky opens up on a hill. The bulging elephant herds of clouds move in, closing fast toward the land. The clouds, low and heavy now, seem to muffle all sound, box everything in with grey fluff walls.

Yes, there is a silence here. Like the pausing of a breath. Just for a moment in eternity.

The youth on the motorcycle backs off on the hand throttle as he crests the hill above Mutton Hollow.

Then, what was going to happen, happened. No one saw this. No person, anyway.

It just happened, and the present drifted into the past and, for a moment, there was no time, just an eternal moment that can't be erased. Ever.

A lone cow, ambling up the slope of the hill, moved onto the road.

The cow was a stray, drifted up from some tucked-away farm well off of the highway. Lonesome, maybe. An adventurer. You see them all the time along these Ozark roads, outside the fences, feeding on the same grass that's inside the fences.

The cow chose just that moment when the Honda rider came careening over the top of the hill, shot down the grade, his pipes bluehot, his engine smoke thin as his carburetor gulped for air and gas like an asthmatic. He hit the cow full on and went over the high side, over the front fender like a man shot from a circus cannon. The handlebar caught his chest like a marlin-spike, horned him like a fighting bull tossing its head.

He twisted in the air like a trampoline artist, moving slow, up and out, over the road and into the cedar-stippled slope below the road. At that moment he was Manolete at his last moment of truth, a bullfighter caught in the afternoon shadows of a terrible ӧcorreoӧ, a lifeless rag doll tossed into the sodden air of summer by a Spanish bull raised on the Miura ranch.

The young man landed breathless in a clump of brush, rolled to a dead stop.

The cow, its hip broken, bawled painfully back into its own country, its nostrils blowing steam, its mouth flecked with foam; bewildered.

The torn and crumpled motorcycle coughed as it choked on its side in the opposite ditch. Its engine died and the metal ticked for a long time as it cooled in its lifelessness, buried in the hulk of the motorcycle sprawled below a dusty cedar tree, as dead as its master.

August Rain

A hundred years ago a man rode over this same spot. He followed a ridge road up from Mutton Hollow, headed for the mighty White River. It was August, and it was hot. He carried a cane fishing pole, an empty peach can full of worms, supper in a lard pail. A rattlesnake twirred a deadly warning from the side of the road. The horse, a dappled mare, spooked, kicked up, bucked. The man, caught unawares, felt his feet fly out of the stirrups. He pitched out of the small saddle with its low cantle, fell down the slope. He struck his head on a rock. For a long time he lay there, staring blindly up at the darkening sky, wondering if he would ever get up. There was pain in his back, and the trees looked fuzzy, distant. Blood leaked down his face and the sky kept darkening until it was blotted out long before sunset. Something strong and iron tightened around his chest and he finally knew he could not breathe anymore.

There is no explanation for these things. They just happen. They happened a hundred years ago, and they happen now. Life is what it is, and it's death, too, and that's part of it, part of a fabric we can't understand. But, life

An Early Frost

is all right, because it shows us things and it seems to go on, through us, the living, and find those to come. And, we remember those who left us for no apparent reason and look for reasons because we know there are reasons. But we don't know what those reasons are and maybe we're not supposed to because it might be that we are supposed to look for reasons to live and learn and find what it is we should find.

Maybe it's the journey that counts. The going over roads. The looking.

And, who's to say what each of us finds along the way? Who among us know?

The people going by are going by, and those who have gone, are gone. Yet, there is something left behind, always, in a smile, a look, a glance. A remembrance. Who touches us, but people? And, who touches people, but something bigger than people? Ah, it's mad August and the hammering sun smashes down and the writing night is as hellish as the smoldering, smothering day. There are not many things I know, but there is much I want to learn.

August Rain

Moments later, the man in the Buick roared past, oblivious to the tragedy that had just occurred, his eyes lit by the grey of sky and the monotonous empty road ahead.

The widow, back at home, saw the rain coming, put out her hand and ran for cover under the porch.

The small boy who had seen the motorcycle pass looked up at the sky and opened his mouth to taste the wet air, wait for a free drink.

The teenaged girl, with her ice cream cone, got into a car with a boy she knew and they drove off to a place they know on Table Rock Lake where there is music and grass and friends, where they can swim and hitch a ride on a boat. A place where they can look into each other's eyes and not have to explain anything in their hearts.

Somewhere, beyond all this, a father begins packing the fishing poles, the tackle boxes into the boat. He looks at the rain sky and thinks of tomorrow. His wife is making potato salad inside the house, thinking of sandwiches, wondering when her boy will be home to bring the cooler in, clean it. In the garage, when she goes there to see her husband, she frowns at the oil spot on the concrete where the Honda sits at night, in the dark, her son's helmet flat upon its black seat.

"Isn't Johnny home yet?" she asks.

"No, not yet," says her husband. "He'll be here directly."

The frown lingers on the woman's face for a long time after she goes back into the house, lingers like the black behemoths in the sky.

The man begins to hum to himself as the sky darkens, darkens.

The hot August rain begins to fall. It drives down hard, falls thick on the hills, the trees, the roads.

The rain drums against the failed armor of the boy's skin. It rattles silver lances against a knight's helmet, moves on, upslope, leaving its fleeting, soothing tracks on the burning asphalt and its misty smoke hanging lifeless in the August air.

BULL SHOALS CAMP

Outside, in the dark, the fishing boats are gliding in to shore, their hulls whispering, hissing. The trailer is very close to the water, windows fogged up from our breath, the heat inside. Rain has misted the lake and this camp all day long. The mist has smeared everything with a dull pewter glaze.

The windows in the little trailer make the things outside appear as if they were protected by a scrim. The picnic tables, the barbecue grills are out of focus. They are that way in the dark, were that way under the grey clouds of afternoon. The chug of outboard motors are muffled by the same damp shroud that envelops us. The mist hangs in veils like sound baffles on a recording stage of yesteryear. Sheets of

An Early Frost

mist from a point of light between two hills end, as far as we know, just beyond this inlet here at Tucker Hollow on Bull Shoals Lake.

My son is asleep on the cushioned seat on the other side of the table. Lights shimmer like luminous ghosts outside our steamed windows. The radio, a lonely sentinel on FM, blares out music snatched out of the air. The music, too, is blurred, distorted.

We have had a good day out in the wind and the rain. There was not much rain. More a drizzle, than anything else. A wetness that stalked across the lake under slowly moving dark clouds. We could see the moisture coming and when it hit us, it was refreshing--a spray against the face, cool and soft as silk. The light drench was brief, no more than a brush of lips in a fleeting kiss.

Marc, my son, has played on the damp swings, slid slowly down the slide. The metal's wetness clung to his small trousers, holding him back. He thought that was quite an odd experience, and so did I. He has been concerned with speed lately, now that he's almost seven years old at the time I write this.

The lake, with its immense face, takes away much of that urgency. Everything seems to move in slow motion here.

There were a couple of small, light planes that flew over today, just under the clouds. They were gnats in slow motion, stuck against the grey sky, lights blinking like lightning bugs, for the longest time. Then, they too, were gone, like the fine mist that strolled across the lake and then disappeared in the smoky trees beyond the shore.

The trailer is warm, cozy. It glows with a friendly orange light. It is easy to think that we are the only people in the world out here. Yet, there are other campers here. Their lights burn like copper halos through our own steamy windows. Fishermen load and unload their trailers. Some men fish only at night. They seem beckoned by some ancient call, some primal tugging of the veins that makes them go out after the sun is down and fish the dark waters.

They, too, must sense the darkness as friend. We do. Marc has no ingrained dread of the dark. His only complaint is that this phenomenon, when we are home, signals the arrival of his bedtime. That's why he likes to camp. We do not look at clocks or watches. The night, then, is a time of blazing campfires, roasting marshmallows, delight in running through the shadowy camp with other children who do not have to go to bed.

His face is so peacefully composed right now, I want to reach under the table to his bunk and touch him. I want to tell him that I understand the rebellions that spring up in his mind like sudden squalls.

He is asleep now because there is school tomorrow. He cannot understand Daylight Savings Time. At 8:30 P.M. it is still light. Still light enough to play. Yet, he must go to bed. The lingering light, and our parental policies, are torture for a young man bursting with life.

It would be better if he could know that we care about his feelings and don't want him to lose a minute of waking life. But, we are hamstrung by tradition. In the morning, if he doesn't go to sleep early, his eyes will be puffy. He will be cranky and pugnacious when he has to be awakened so that I can drive him back home to get ready for school.

Somewhere, somewhere along the way, we lost sight of some things. Maybe, of everything important. We created jobs and built empires. We worked and acquired land. We began to possess things that we manufactured. We made watches and time clocks. We made charts and graphs. We stockpiled arms and wasted food. We dug and mined and kept building. Higher and higher, longer and farther. We raced the universe, knowing we would lose. The universe is a slow, inexorable entity that expands and contracts like a breathing lung. We thought we could beat it to the end of time, to the end of death. Instead, we found that the universe is curved, and just keeps going on and on, endlessly. It is in no hurry.

So, Marc sleeps here under a fogged window, unaware of these movements within the vast universe beyond our night. He has a faint inkling of space travel when he swings high in the playground. He has an intimation of speed when he hurtles down the slick steel slide. He knows the motion of planets and stars and galaxies when he spins on the merry-go-round. These playthings serve, perhaps, as little reminders of our past, our future, our certain

An Early Frost

hitch to the universe. We spin and slide and glide through space and our blood churns like the sea, rises and falls in a tide surge with the pulling force of our own close moon. Something inside us knows where we came from. We do not know where we are going.

The glass of our future is smeared, fogged over. We can see little glimmers of light. Orange halos, yellow pinpoints in the fabric of dark. Far off glows of other worlds.

Perhaps that is enough for us now. We are cozy inside our trailer. We can travel a bit. We can see new places, explore unknown vistas of the mind. We can drift a bit on our mortal tether.

And, every time we think we know the answers to all the eternal questions, there will be a sheet of fine mist stalking across space to blur our eyes, to splash us with simple rays of truth.

The lake seems huge and endless now. In the dark, it is barely navigable. We sit in the trailer and that becomes our universe. For now. We are not chained here, however. We can move. We can go on and on.

There is a beauty to the travel of mind and body. For every mystery that is bared, exposed, another presents itself.

The mystery is in the glass, in the fog-breath on the windows, in the magical peach-glow of lamps that throw stripes across the shore, bleeding ribbons on the water. The men in boats are out there, too, peering into the light-smeared lake, looking for something alive and shining that they cannot see.

Tomorrow, we will hitch up the trailer and go back home.

There is irony there, of course. The trailer is our home. Or has been for a couple of days.

It is temporary, but in the ways of the universe, it is as temporary as the earth itself, although some say it will last forever.

The wonder is that, every so often, for the fisherman, there is a dynamic tug on the line, a mighty, brief struggle, just before something marvelous and silver breaks free of the lake, dances above the masked depths trying to shake the hook that jarred it loose from its hidden world.

Outside, in the dark, there is movement. I peer through the damp fog on the window glass. I see a ripple of waters, the shape of a man moving along the shore. There is a sudden flash of lightning. For a second, I see everything outside clearly. A moment later, it is pitch dark again. The thunder rattles the windows of the trailer.

Marc, asleep, has seen none of this.

But, someday, he will. He will be awake when such things happen. I hope that he will begin to wonder, as I do, and to take comfort in existence. Not existence as ideal or perfection, but existence as a gift, as wonderment.

Again, thunder. As it rolls across the lake, reverberates on the waters and rockets into a muffled roar over the hills, it sounds something like human speech, magnified billions of times.

Someday, when Marc is a man, I hope that speech becomes conversation.

Someday, I hope he will be one of those fishermen out there in the dark.

RAGE AGAINST THE DYING

He did not tell me he was dying.

Instead, he said that parts of his body were dying, shutting down, one by one.

I loved this man. He had a very fine mind that he exercised in a very capable way through his writing, through the many projections of his strong personality. His mind, I think, was a projection of his soul, a palpable extension of his eternal spirit.

Two weeks before he died, we talked about his death, and mine. We spoke in terms of reality and in terms of ideas. Which are often one and the same, to employ a useful cliche. We sat together at a table in a small tavern, in dim light, with other writers around us.

An Early Frost

None of the others heard us talking, and that was to our benefit. What we had to say was not necessarily pleasant, but it was necessary. I will not presume to call this man a close friend, only because the ways of judging friendships are complex. I had long admired this man's writing, and since meeting him, the admiration went deeper, because he spoke more in person than he did in his writing.

I have never been to his house, he has never been to mine. But, that is the way, sometimes, with writers. We work alone and we think alone, in terms of human relationships, and when we go out in public, we present ourselves as normal human beings, the work of our minds lying on a desk or in a drawer at home, out of sight.

The man, let's call him Gent, as in gentle, as in gentleman, as in gentry, as in genesis, as in gen--a prefix for mankind, appeared very frail, very gaunt, from the ravages of physical illnesses that tore at his body. His complexion lacked the vital color of the outdoor life he had lived. He was pale, skeletal, in the subdued light of the small tavern. I touched his arm and it was thin as a broomstick, his shoulders were sharp as axe-blades and he struggled for breath like an asthmatic.

"Jory," he told me, "I am dying."

Yes, I thought, as I looked into his haunted eyes. But, that was not enough for me.

"What do you mean?" I asked.

"Oh," he said, with a breathless scrape of gravel in his voice, "I can feel parts of me shutting down. The organs. One after another."

"Have you thought about dying? About how it would be, what you would face when it all goes dark?"

"Some," Gent said laconically.

"I have thought about it, too. A lot. I have a disease called apnea. Have you ever heard about it?"

"No, I can't say as I have," he said, his eyes bright for a moment as if the hot sun beamed straight into his face.

"Whenever I lie down to sleep, my breath shuts off. It just shuts off cold and I rise up, gasping, struggling for air. It is a terrible thing. There is no rational explanation for it."

An Early Frost

"I see," he said. "Breathing is life. If something interferes, you grow weak. Life is then something that is mortal."

"Yes. Well, what is happening to you? You see yourself failing at every moment. Does it bother you?"

"Yes," he said, "it bothers me."

"Why?"

"It seems so damned unfair," said Gent.

"But, it is not you that is dying. It is only your body, a temporary dwelling place, a residence for your soul."

Gent looked at me hard and long.

"Do you feel old?" I asked. "I mean, inside?"

"No, not that way. I feel old with my body letting me down."

"That is something I've been wrestling with for a long time. You are the same age as you always were. It shows in your writing, in your eyes, in your talk, in your personality. Inside, at our centers, we are ageless. We are young."

"I think you may be right," he said. "My mind does not feel age. The dying, the shutting down of one organ after another, annoys me.

I don't want to die this way. Piece by piece. My body is letting me down and there's nothing I can do about it."

"These bodies we have. They are only machines. We drive them, we use them, but like all machines, they fail us, Gent. They break down, they collapse. This is what is happening to you and me. We are not old. Our spirits are young, we are constantly learning."

He looked at me, his eyes restless, pensive.

I didn't know if Gent agreed with me. It was something I had thought about over the years, wondering why our bodies aged and our minds did not. Was this part of man's eternal spirit, and ivisible, yet finite part of our being? I have thought about it a lot and I wonder if this is all there is. Why are we here? This is a question everyone asks at one point in life, at least, either consciously or subconsciously. If life means nothing, why live it? If it does mean something, then what does it mean?

Gent leaned closer to me, and put his hand atop mine.

"Go on," he said.

An Early Frost

"When I was a boy," I told him, "I thought of emptiness a lot, of nothingness. I mean, I lay on my back in a southern clay field and looked up at the empty sky and thought of the world before it was a world. It scared the hell out of me and I felt very alone. Later in life, I felt lost and helpless. That was because I had not looked deeply enough into myself, into the earth, into the universe. But, as I did, and this was after coming close to death on several occasions, I saw a meaning, a purpose."

"Yes, I know," Gent said softly.

"We are here to learn. Just as the universe, as every creature and atom in it, learns. We grow out of our early selves into other beings, other extensions of life that we probably will never understand. Yet, back of it, each of us is the baby, the child, wide-eyed and innocent, eternal."

"That is the majestic aspect of life," said Gent. "Nothing is ever destroyed. Only transformed."

"Inside your machine," I said, "you are the driver, the same bright mind that glows and pulses like the stars, the power just as strong as it ever was. You will leave this old body behind, but I believe you, that which is your mind, your personality, that which is spirit, is deathless, indestructible, timeless, as eternal as the universe."

"Maybe you're right," he said. "Who's to challenge your own beliefs, who's to say that this is not really the way things are according to your own conception of life and death?"

"Maybe. I don't know. It seems such a waste, to put us here, have us live, suffer and die, learn some things and then just be obliterated as though we never existed. Look, Gent, I just can't believe that a God, a Great Spirit, would let this happen. But, a long time ago, when I was faced with my own death, I came to grips with this issue and to a conclusion that, if not comforting, at least resolves all these matters to my satisfaction."

"And, what is that?" Gent asked me, his voice very low and raspy.

"We are all part of a vast, complex system. We are in worlds within worlds and nothing is stable. Yet, beneath the chaos there is a strange kind of order and this order is something conscious and reasonable. Sometimes

An Early Frost

it cannot be measured and even if we do measure it, it makes no sense to our finite minds. It matters to us, while we're alive, to understand these rhythms and harmonies in the turbulence of life and nature and the universe. But it doesn't really matter what we think may happen to us. Something is going to happen and we cannot imagine what it is except in corporal terms. The body dies, it turns to acid, it becomes something else. If we live beyond this mortal coil, this weary, troublesome life, in some form, then maybe that is all to the good. It means we have the chance to go on learning, to discover, to improve ourselves, refine our thinking. I don't mean reincarnation, in the popular sense, but I mean existing, becoming, stretching out, being. We leave order and enter chaos and in chaos there is beauty and refinement of another kind. That is one side of it.

"If there is nothing, if there is no life after death, if we just die and our minds go blank, our personalities wiped out, then what does it matter? If there is nothing, there is nothing. We just had this time for ourselves and there is no memory, no hope, no promise, no life after this life, and death, as well as life, is totally meaningless. A shame, but then there is nothing to worry about, is there? We will be as if we had never lived. But, the universe won't. We will have made some small changes that may not manifest themselves for billions of years in some galaxy beyond our sight."

"Pascal," Gent said quietly. "The poet, the mathematician. He said a similar thing once."

"What a tragic waste. I can't believe that this is the way it will be, but either way, there is nothing to worry about, nothing to fear."

Gent laughed and that mischievous, wise brilliance danced in his eyes. I could see that he had come to terms with his own dying and that it was a private, secret belief that he would carry with him to his final mortal resting place.

I have thought about this conversation a lot since that afternoon. When I wrote this down, Gent was still alive, in the hospital. His body was wrinkled, thin, failing him. There was chaos in his body. The machine was winding down, behaving erratically, breaking up, piece by piece. But, that body was only a housing for his soul, in this world, on this earth, and it had served its purpose. I did not think that Gent was dying. I thought that only the vehicle he drove through life was rusting away. He would go on to better things, if my hunch was correct. Yet, I feel as all who cherish life do--there will be an emptiness here, a vacant space in our universe. And, something inside me, the human part of my soul, cries out as Dylan Thomas cried out in anguish over the death of his father: "Rage, rage," he wrote, "against the dying of the light."

I raged too, Gent, against the dying of your light.

But, energy can neither be created nor destroyed. It can only be transformed. I do not believe that you, your fine young strong eternal spirit will ever die.

I believe your light will shine, somewhere, forever.

AFTER MANY A SUMMER

He floated out to Little Elbow, the motor chugging soft, the prop chortling in the still waters. The lake was flawless that afternoon, a smoky mirror reflecting the white puffs of clouds sailing slow as spring white geese across a blue sky. Images of bluffs and dull green cedars daubed the depths near the far shore. He always told people: "you get two pieces of scenery for the price of one," and sometimes when he looked down at the water painting he forgot about the other world, the one made of rock and wood and earth. The one made of pain and disease and death. Jess cut the Mercury engine, drifted in the silence. The boat plowed through the glassy sheet that wrinkled as he passed. In the reflection, the towering stone bluffs rippled like ancient shrines toppling in slow motion.

The deck boat slowed to a halt in the airless calm. The sun would be down soon. It hovered just above the tallest western ridge, boiling with flame. Jess watched as the last wavelet slapped against the rock-strewn shore, disappeared. A blue heron stood stately as a statue on one of the bluff's outcroppings, its head cocked to focus a single pale eye on the water below. A red-tailed hawk floated on a current of air just above the wild orchard of berried cedars, quiet water oaks, scaley-barked hickory trees. Farther off, on another plane high above the hawk, a turkey buzzard soared in widening circles, riding its invisible carousel with lazy grace, gliding on the thermals with only an occasional lackadaisical flick of feathered wing-tips.

"Mr. Arneson," Doctor Kruger had said to him that morning, "it's spreading rapidly now. In a day or so you won't be able to stand the pain. In a week or so...." He had used other words, big words, ugly words. Jess knew what they meant, but he couldn't pronounce them, couldn't say them aloud to himself.

Kruger had wanted him to go into the hospital, but Jess had refused. Not now. Not yet. Not while the summer was in full bloom. He had enough pain pills to stun the agony, dull its rage. He could grit it out for a week or two.

He didn't want to go out that way, lying in a strange bed with white sheets and the smell of medicine and disease in his nostrils.

For some time his body had been shutting down. Piece by piece. He pasted a nitroglycerine patch near his heart every day to keep his heart pumping. He took pills to hold down his blood pressure. Procardia. Capoten. One of his kidneys was no longer functioning. The other was shooting renin into his bloodstream in a frantic attempt to survive. The kidney, Kruger had said, would save itself at all costs if threatened. It would attempt to survive at the expense of the brain, putting him in danger of experiencing what Kruger euphemistically referred to as "a cerebral cardiovascular event." A massive stroke.

The cancer, Jess thought ironically, was almost an afterthought. He was falling apart. Piece by piece.

The hawk disappeared, swallowed up in secret by the trees and sheer distance. The heron stretched its wings, struggled off its platform, ungainly for a brief moment, its pinions straining to build up a cushion of air. Then, airborne, it flew gracefully across the arm of the lake toward a distant mudflat at the far end of Little Elbow.

There were bass lurking in the waters below the bluffs, Jess knew. He could no longer cast for them. He could hold a pole and fish for crappie, but the schools were scattered now, gone from the brush, the sunken cedar skeletons he had set out for them. The bottom of the boat was littered with plastic jugs. Each jug had his name and address on a scrap of paper in it, his Cedar Creek telephone number. Each jug was wrapped with twelve feet of heavy line, the line weighted with washers and nuts two feet above the single snelled hook. This was the way Jess fished now. He set the jugs out each evening, baiting the hooks with live crawdads, silvery shad minnows, or small fluttering bluegills.

In the morning, if there was another morning for him, he would track down the jugs, take in his catch. One or two catfish a day, he'd been averaging, the ten and twelve pound flatheads or the channel cats, food for him and his few friends.

Many a Summer

Jess had thought about how he wanted to go out. Not in bed, but on the lake. Like one of his Viking ancestors. All he had to do was take enough pills, soak the deck with gasoline and, just before the darkness grasped him, strike a match. A floating funeral pyre, a fitting finish for a man of the lake, for a man descended from Norse warriors.

Jess started the motor with a push of a button. He could no longer pull the cord, so he had installed the electric starter. He rammed the tiller arm over hard, twisted the throttle. He aimed for the setting sun, set his course for his favorite channel. When he rounded the point, he began to bait the hooks. He tossed the jugs over the side, saw them bob like tiny mines in the wake of his boat.

If he did not pick up the jugs in the morning, he would miss the thrill of tracking them down, pulling up fish. He would miss that rush of adrenalin when he saw a jug go under, bob back up, flashing in the morning sun. It seemed pointless to set them out if he was to miss the morning hunt with the cool breeze fresh against his face. He might come up empty; he might pull in a beauty. There was a wonder to such fishing; a magic. Just as there was to life.

Summers past bobbed up in his memory. He remembered getting into the white bass on Beaver Creek early one morning during a late spawn. He could cast his line, then, and a white rooster tail on 4 lb. test dragged next to a gravel point brought him all the excitement and action he could handle for 45 minutes. He filled his stringer that morning and in the afternoon, he found crappie at twenty feet on Bull Shoals, floating in the brush like sunken zepplins.

Another time, he threw crank bait at a rocky shore, snaked the lure through brush in the shallows and watched the water boil with a 10 lb. bigmouth bass. A few yards away, another bass shredded the water as he danced on his tail trying to shake the treble hook from his massive jaw. That fish had gone eight pounds and the next weighed in at six. Even now, he knew a place where the bass came up to a waterfall looking for worms and all he had to do was drop a line over the side, dangle a nightcrawler about ten feet down, and the big ones would come to the bait like sharks on a blood hunt.

And, strangely, he remembered the Trumpeters. For a time, when he was a boy, they lived on a small lake and every Fall the Trumpeter Swans would come down from the north. He loved those huge, stately birds, loved to watch them gliding on the lake like Viking ships. Once, he had asked his mother if the swans did not live forever.

"No," she told him. "They die. But they go somewhere, to a secret place, where they die with dignity. No one knows where they go."

Suddenly, a great sadness cloaked him, smothered him. Did he have the courage, the determination, to crush all hope, to wipe out tomorrow with the striking of a match? It seemed, then, an arrogance, a blasphemous affront to the mysterious Almighty, if there was such, who had given him, had given all things, life. With that life, he had been given the power to make choices, even in the matter of life and death.

The true test of a man, he thought, rested in his ability to make the right decisions. Yet the pain could temper that ability. The pain could make him its slave, stripping his spirit of all affinity to the divine. What was life anyway, but learning? Perhaps the pain was something he was supposed to see before he died. Perhaps the pain was there to teach him something.

When he had set the last jug, he headed for his homely, weathered dock, his jaw set in determination. He had not lived as a cheater. He would not die as one. These last few years had been peaceful, not dramatic. He saw no reason to change the way he lived by trying to change the way he died. Was not death a part of life, something to be faced bravely? A Viking could look death in the face. So could he. No pills. No gasoline. Fish until he could no longer get in the boat, wait patiently for the last jug of memory to bob out of sight.

As he crossed the main arm of the lake, the sun held just over the high ridges for a long moment. It set the water afire, and the boat glowed in the cool magical flames of a Missouri sunset. Jess Arneson drew himself up straight, his gnarled, liver-spotted hand gentle on the throttle, his craggy Scandinavian face burnished ruddy by the sun, smudges of shadows under the cheekbones, in the hollows around his blue eyes.

In the center of the lake, the summer blossomed one last time that day. Jess cut the motor, exulting in that moment. His boat floated in fire; its twin shimmered in the ripples, in the watery mirror. All afire, sailing soundlessly into the endless sunset like a Viking ship, like an elegant swan aflame.

Jess smiled and his fierce countenance softened. This was the way, he said to himself. This was the way. Ride it out. Ride all the way into the sunset, the darkness beyond. Ride the lake until the last embers faded, turned to ashes in the sky.

Die with grace, like a swan.

THE TREES

It is hard not to think of the trees here in these hills as friends.

I hear them in the morning as they sing their green songs. I shake hands with them after I have had my half cup of coffee sometime after dawn. They make me smell good after a night's sleep. It must be that their fragrance seeps through the open windows and soaks into my flesh during the night. These are the cedars I'm talking about. They are everywhere on this jungled farmstead, all sizes, shapes, and personalities.

Some are big enough to make you feel small. Some are young and tender, afraid of being turned into fence posts, kindling, chests, walls, Christmas trees. Some of them are gnarled by the wind, homely in their bending.

On the high ground above our small pond, they get the brunt of the hard weather and heavy snows that flock their branches in winter. Others are confident and smiling, arrogant toward the deciduous oaks and hickorys that stand as towering neighbors. Still others are comfortable, like old chairs, happy to have us stroll among them, glad to have us sit sheltered in their shade.

These cedars are special to me, with their rough, scratchy fingers. Yet their touch is as comforting as any delicate hand. When they are laden with the tiny blueberries, they seem proud and pregnant, radiating a silent reverence for life.

Some of the old cedars bear scars. These wounds hurt when you touch them, because the imagination is more powerful than sight. I have seen the cedars bleed their amber blood, seen the sap eke out, catch the sun until, saturated with light, it shines like a jewel.

In their soft songs, when their branches are played by the wind, the cedars are green-gowned ladies in a Victorian garden; in their deep-throated bass humming, they are stately gentlemen in chorus, stalwart singers of a time gone by in a faraway land.

On a spring morning like this, the trees are almost ambulatory in the shift of light. They seem to move like veridian chess pieces in the forest, fragrantly subtle, and with great feeling, a feeling that surges through you when you come close, listen.

A periwinkle sky and the hills shimmering in the sun conspire to light the cedars up like aquamarine candles. Green fire, like a million emeralds shattered into shards, splinters over the ridges, the slopes, until even the hollows blaze with a dazzling light. Heady scents scrawl invisible tracks down the slopes on vagrant zephyrs that thread through this valley, transform it into a constantly changing tapestry of wildwood.

I have seen these humble cedars sleeping at night under a full moon as though they were statues of people in a garden. I have felt them whisper against my fences in the darkness, swaying green islets floating anchorless towards shore. It's an affirmation of life to see them stolid in the dark, pewtered to a dull silver by the moon, a shelter for birds and beasts, a haven for life both wild and tame.

I like the cedars because they are not native to the Ozarks. Because they are considered homely and useless, and because they grow so fast and so thick on these hills, not many people like them. I do. I like them because I can see into their hearts and remember my mother's cedar chest and the soft colors of the wood grain, striated like a western sunset. I like them because they give up their full fragrance only when they are dead. Their aromatic scent lingers for generations.

Do the cedars pirouette in circles like ballerinas in the dusk? Do they surge up and down the hills, or stand, still as sentinels, for eternity?

I don't know.

Light is shadow, color is shadow, Goethe believed, and perhaps he was right. We cannot see all that exists, we can only determine existence through our senses and through intuition. Shadows of things, hidden windows in the fabric of a complicated, tumultuous universe.

An Early Frost

The cedars move for me, in and out of time, deciding memory, captivating thought, stirring desire, roiling up unseen things for the eyes to probe, prodding the deepest instincts of the restless, searching mind. I rub their cocoon-like bark and feel the sting of their needles.

I breathe of them and breathe of time past.

I think of the cedar trees here as friends. Newcomers, like me. Yet, here to stay as long as seeds blow in the wind, settle and take root in the soil.

They produce no edible fruit nor nuts nor berries. Cedars are the weeds of the tree kingdom. They are homely and not suitable to build frame houses. People chop them up and use pieces of them for little souvenir boxes or to line chests with in order to kill moth larvae.

To hear some people talk, no one would miss them if they were suddenly uprooted, taken from the Ozarks.

I would miss them.